Alaskans Die Young

Susan Hudson Johnson

McRoy & Blackburn
Publishers

Elmer E. Rasmuson Library Cataloging in Publication Data:

Johnson, Susan Hudson.

Alaskans die young / Susan Hudson Johnson.
Ester, Alaska : McRoy & Blackburn, c2005.

  p. cm.

ISBN 0-9706712-37

1. Alaska—Fairbanks—Fiction. 2. Detective and mystery
stories, American—Alaska—Fairbanks. I. Title.

PS3610.O382 A43 2005

McRoy and Blackburn, Publishers
PO Box 276
Ester, Alaska 99725
www.alaskafiction.com

Book and cover design and layout by Sue and Russ Mitchell, Inkworks.

Acknowledgements

My heartiest thanks to Lael Morgan, in whose writing class I began working on this book and who said I wrote like Washington Irving; to Jean Anderson, who critiqued the book ten years ago, remembered it, and one year ago, recommended it to publisher Carla Helfferich; to Carla, a hard taskmaster and a delight to work with; to Pat Babcock and Gene Kuhn, who extricated the book from ancient computer files; to Leone Hatch, who spent hours untangling my self-inflicted computer glitches; and to Jana Peirce, Nancy Kuhn, and Judy Jackson, who came when I needed them.

The irrepressible grandson, Andrew, is a composite character created from happy memories of one nephew, Andrew; five sons, Richard, Eric, Alex, Rob, and Charlie; and one granddaughter, Suz. Thank you all ... I think.

The Oysters actually existed, but not as presented here. The original Oysters, who also met in months with an *R*, were members of the Fairbanks branch of the American Association of University Women. There is absolutely no similarity between the members of the Oysters as described in *Alaskans Die Young* and the original AAUW group, who disbanded many years ago.

Beyond these faint congruencies, all characters described in these pages are purely fictional. Opinions expressed by Heather Adams are not necessarily those of the author.

The quotations at the beginnings of chapters are from *The Man Who Made Friends With Himself,* by Christopher Morley.

Chapter 1

Put the whole of life on a sundial in April. Reckon by sunlight only. Oysters go out of season and poets in.

Aristotle said a story should have a beginning, a middle, and an end. Actually, he said "tragedy," which this story certainly is, although some might say that it is detective fiction, a horror story, a murder mystery, even a comedy. I'm still not sure when, or where, this story began. I'm not sure it has entirely come to an end, and I have not yet come to terms with its middle. I only know that it began for me a year ago, in another April, at the last meeting of my writing club, the Oysters, before we closed down for the summer. We call ourselves the Oysters because we meet only in months with an *R*.

I was a little late. On the way to the meeting I couldn't resist stopping at the old Creamer's Dairy Farm, now a wildlife sanctuary, for a few minutes to watch the migrating Canada geese, ducks, swans, and cranes as they circled the field and plunked themselves down among their brethren. When I finally arrived at Marian Aldrich's big log house, the other Oysters, all eight, were present and busy serving themselves Sara Lee cheesecake and Sanka. After tactfully guiding Gwendolyn Williams to a sturdy chair, Marian, our president, opened the meeting by reminding everyone that this would be our last gathering of the Oysters until September, which has an *R*. She laughed her little "heh, heh," at her joke, which is rather old by now. She looked around the room to see if anyone was joining her. They looked more pained than amused.

The first order of business was the matter of submissions; every month we report on manuscripts sent out and returned, rejected. In the seventeen years we've been meeting, we have had only a dozen or so acceptances, and I won't speculate on the number of rejections. We all have thick folders of those awful printed slips. So far, our only successes have been a primer on gardening in the far north, a few short stories, some magazine articles on cat care, and half a dozen love poems. But we all continue our writing, undaunted. You have to admire a group as dedicated as that.

We have no set order of reading, except that Katie George, a Koyukon Indian and our only Alaska-born member, always has her hand up first. Katie left both her husband and the Oysters two years ago. She never explained, and we never asked, but five months ago she suddenly returned, highly motivated and much more friendly and outgoing than she'd ever been before. She immediately presented her plan: to write her autobiography, *Daughter of the Yukon.* Every month she has presented one or more chapters, and her determination is a lesson to all of us, although, she says, it's really the other way around; our determination inspires her.

Katie has a little Russian blood from the original invaders, which may account for her taller-than-average height for an Indian woman. In her midforties, she has long, shiny black hair, tonight hanging loose down her back, but sometimes restrained in braids and beads. Her burnished bronze skin, surprising for a person whose ancestors have lived through ten thousand or more long sunless arctic winters, is wrinkle free, and her strong, athletic body exudes energy. She used to be a woman of few words, but lately, for reasons unknown, she has become not only more chatty but sometimes even funny.

Katie passed out three copies of chapter nine of *Daughter of the Yukon*; each page was quickly read and passed on. Soon everyone was busy reading and taking notes. She wrote, from the perspective of an adolescent Katie, of the hardships of a large family living in a crowded cabin, in winter chopping firewood to feed the iron stove, hacking through river ice to dip water; and in summer picking berries, fishing, preserving food, and stashing wood for the return of the great cold, which sometimes outlasted their hard-won supplies.

When every Oyster had finished reading the final page, there was a moment of silence and then an outpouring of genuine enthusiasm.

"At the September meeting," announced Katie, "I'll be taking orders for my book."

Eight Oysters stared at her, open mouthed.

"Want to bet?" laughed Katie.

Florence Hokkainen was next. Almost six feet tall and broad shouldered, she must be well into her seventies, but she doesn't look it. A commanding presence, she's always expensively coiffed, gowned, and bejeweled. Her neon-auburn hair, her purple satin and velvet dresses, and her flashy diamonds make her the center of attention wherever she goes. There are persistent rumors that Florence used to run a brothel in Anchorage, and obviously she's had a lot of business experience somewhere; but she says she was in the catering business and that she retired after she married one of her clients, an elderly Finn who'd struck it rich gold mining. Florence has been a wealthy widow for many years.

When we first started the Oysters, Florence naturally assumed that with her business experience she was the Oyster most qualified to run the organization. We held our monthly meetings in each others houses, then as now, and at first we appreciated Florence's willingness to offer her house and to preside over our meetings. Soon all meetings were being held at Florence's luxurious Victorian residence, presided over by Florence, and the rest of us began to feel as if Florence were the madam and we were her "girls."

Every meeting was a display of silver and china and every "light repast" was enough to feed a dozen iron workers. We finally had to vote in a new set of bylaws decreeing that we must all take turns being president of the Oysters, in alphabetical order, and likewise, we must all take turns being hostess, in reverse alphabetical order. We also outlawed the sumptuous spreads and replaced them with an unvarying menu of Sara Lee cheesecake and Sanka.

Florence still takes a dim view of our limited menu and, being the self-appointed mistress of protocol, a post from which we can't remove her, she frequently demonstrates her disdain for the casual dress style, i.e., recycled or secondhand, of some of the members, and she hates vulgar language. Every time I say "dump," she mutters "landfill."

Florence, like Katie, is writing her autobiography. So far she has been a year getting from Seattle to Valdez on the Alaska Steamship Line, and three months getting from Valdez to Anchorage, although the original bus trip only took a day and a half. Her current installment didn't hasten the trip at all; I'm not sure she really wants to reach Anchorage. Naturally her work was graciously accepted, but we all wish she would get on with her story.

Abbie Buffmire, in her sixties, is just a little thing. Wiry and agile as a monkey, she's a retired elementary school teacher and our only successful author—the book on gardening, which she self-published. She not only does most of the work in her huge vegetable and flower gardens, she practically built her own house, single-handed. The late Mr. Buffmire (as Abbie affectionately refers to him) was not a practical man; I don't believe he even owned a screwdriver before they were married. Abbie did her best to teach him some plumbing and electrical work, but he had no aptitude at all. Sadly, not long after he retired from his job as a librarian at the Noel Wien Library, wearied of competing with Abbie's earthworms for attention, he quietly turned up his toes one cold night and breathed his last. Soon afterwards Abbie moved the worms and Arthur the goldfish, who wintered in a plastic garbage barrel, into the space vacated by the late Mr. Buffmire.

Abbie's flower and vegetable gardens and her greenhouses are so spectacular that every summer busloads of tourists come to visit them. Her winters are spent researching new varieties of plants and writing a sequel to her popular book, *The Arctic Gardener.* Winters are also the time for making renovations to her house, adding a room here, a porch there. She passes out starters of worms the way other people pass out sourdough starter. I love to watch Florence's face during our April meetings, when this takes place; her nose actually twitches.

Abbie gave us a brief outline of the chapter she's currently writing. She said it is too technical for us to understand, being aimed at the master gardener. But she did bring the worms.

Marcia Wayman, the next author to share her work, is a tall, angular figure who dresses only in white. She is probably in her mid-forties; one can hardly imagine that she was ever young, nor has she aged a day in seventeen years. She wears her bottle-blond hair in a coronet of braids and uses no makeup. She lives very simply and frugally in a small log cabin off Yankovich Road. Never married, she works as a secretary in the biology department at the University of Alaska. Sometimes I wonder if the Oysters provide the only excitement in her apparently uneventful life.

There is an aura of strength and decisiveness about her, and she has a rather sardonic sense of humor. Perhaps that is what drives her, whenever we meet in her cabin, to place a bottle or two of hard liquor with the usual offerings. No one ever touches it, and if she means to be funny, her effort is wasted

She sees herself as a latter-day Emily Dickinson, writing love poems to her lost, unattainable (or imaginary?) lover. Like her idol, she keeps her poems tied in ribbons in a top bureau drawer, and those not published during her lifetime (she has actually published a few) are to be published posthumously.

Marcia read a heart-wrenching poem about a sad little bird, "Sparrow in the Snow," all alone out in the cold, but we knew the little bird was really Marcia herself.

Sometimes I think the members of the club are more like clams than Oysters. Katie George is not the only secretive one. Perhaps *private* is a better word. Marian Aldrich, our hostess, is a private person too. She is reticent about her personal life, but we have a pretty good idea of what it's like. She used to be a nurse; that's how she met Doctor—she calls her husband Doctor—and life with Doctor is no bed of roses. Doctor lives in one wing of their house and Marian lives in the other. He spends weekends in their luxurious cabin at Birch Lake, where no ladies are invited.

Marian, in her sixties, is sweet faced and soft spoken. She does not appear to be a strong character, and yet she has managed to put up with Doctor for at least twenty years. I've often wondered if it is Doctor's occasional presence, or his habitual absence, that contribute to her general air of uncertainty. There are only two things she's really certain about: one, that she will never leave Doctor, and two, that we must save the planet by recycling every possible item. She is quietly and stubbornly committed to using no more than her share of the planet's resources, so she buys everything secondhand. She does, however, squander some of Doctor's hard-earned money on membership in the local health club, one thing she can't buy secondhand. She is an award-winning weight-lifter in her age group, and her gray hair is maintained at the local beauty school, where she allows the students to experiment on her at will.

I especially enjoy her sense of humor, which, I think, is nonexistent. Whenever someone tells a joke or makes a humorous remark, I look over at Marian, who is usually looking around the room for some indication of whether she should smile, or laugh, or remain uncommitted. Her dry "heh, heh" is heard long after everyone else has finished laughing, when she's quite sure that what she just heard was a joke. Although I'm not absolutely sure she knows what a joke is.

Marian said she's researching an article on recycling, but she had nothing to share that night.

Joan Van Blarcom, also in her forties, is another private Oyster. She's a tall, willowy blond whose golden hair quietly turned to platinum when we weren't looking. Always slim, she is now almost wraithlike. One would never guess that years ago she owned and flew her own Cessna 180 airplane and that she took part in many daring searches and rescues.

Two years ago, like Katie George, she left her husband of twenty-odd years, a biology professor at the university. I'm sure there's no connection. Joan moved out of their house with just what she could carry in a couple of suitcases. There's been no divorce, and there doesn't appear to be any third party involved.

What happened to that vibrant creature? What a strange experience, watching a fellow human being, whom you once thought you knew fairly well, suffering through some kind of cataclysmic life experience and being unable to help her.

Joan, who is the registrar at the University of Alaska, never left the Oysters; instead she increased her authorship of children's stories, which she never, ever, sends out to publishers.

Her latest story was about a little girl who entered her own one-dog team in a children's race, and when her dog got sick, put him in the sled and pulled him all the way to the finish line, which, although not a great distance, was a long way for her. The little girl received a special award, and Joan got lots of praise from us.

There's little mystery about the Williams sisters, although none of us can figure out why one identical twin is skinny as a rail and the other is, well, extremely obese. They own Kollege Kitty Kare, where they board cats for traveling Fairbanksans. Because Florence Hokkainen claims to be allergic to cats, the Oysters never meet in the Williams house, which is strongly redolent of cat, as are, to a lesser extent, Gwladys (never omit the *w*), Gwendolyn, and the departing guest. Everyone is grateful for Florence's allergy, although no one believes in it for a minute.

Gwladys read a short, poignant piece about taking her cat, Winston, to the vet to be put down. He had been querulous and incontinent for months, the cat, not the vet, but Gwladys was quite teary-eyed as she finished the sad tale.

Marcia Wayman created a bit of *contretemps* by suggesting that Gwladys could have saved some money by snuffing the cat herself. I thought the twins would explode. Marcia apologized, and we resumed.

Next, and last, came that indefatigable writer, Heather Adams, *moi,* whose life is an open book. My husband, Rowland, who worked for the Fish and Wildlife Department, disappeared while flying over the Brooks Range thirty years ago; his plane was never found. I raised our son Rowe alone, supporting us by teaching junior high school English. Now retired, I live in a rambling, decrepit old log house, where I am frequently visited by my ten-year-old grandson, Andrew, and his cronies.

I passed out copies of "Final Pitch," a short suspense story about a woman who divorced her domineering and unfaithful husband, winning custody of her two small sons. The ex-husband keeps trying to persuade the woman to return to him, to the point of harassment. One day he asks her to take a short drive with him, to discuss reconciliation one last time. If she refuses, he promises he will bother her no more. Against her better judgment, she goes with him, and her little dog jumps into the car after her. When the ex-husband complains that the dog is drooling, she removes a small rubber ball from its mouth and drops it into her shirt pocket. The ex-husband drives to a state park with a picnic site overlooking a steep drop-off. He parks the car, and over her objections, takes out a basket lunch.

She leaves the car, and, walking over to the cliff edge, looks out over the vast expanse of wilderness. When her ex-husband offers her a drink, she refuses and insists he come to the point. She returns to the car and waits, standing by the closed door. He walks over to the drop-off, and standing on a rotting chunk of log, makes his final pitch: she *must* come back to him; the other woman means nothing to him, he has broken with her. His ex-wife refuses, and opens the car door.

Giving up at last, and balancing lightly on the log, he tells her she has just forfeited her life: he was now going to kill her by faking her accidental death. He proceeds to explain how: he will pick her up, carry her to the edge of the cliff, and drop her off. Then he will obliterate his footsteps with some rags he has brought with him, leaving only hers.

"You can't outwit me, and you can't outrun me," he tells her. He lifts his foot to move toward her. She draws back her arm, and with *her* "final pitch," she hurls the ball at him, striking him in the middle of his forehead. He loses his balance, and, arms extended, falls backward, out over the steep face of the drop-off. His voice, calling her name, fades away in the distance, until there is only silence. She picks up the rubber ball as it rebounds, returns it to her shirt pocket, and calling her little dog, gets into the car and drives off.

The Oysters praised the story extravagantly. They declared it the best thing I had ever written. How many times have I heard that? Why did I listen to them? Well, I got carried away. Inspired and energized, I announced that I was going to write a full-length mystery novel.

As I look back, I keep wondering what would have happened if I had simply said, "Thank you," and let it go at that. But it was April, and I was too big for my britches. In the following months I would find myself not only writer, but detective, suspect, criminal, and victim. My writing, which for so long had never come to anything, suddenly came to something. It came to more than I could handle. But I couldn't stop.

Chapter 2

If I were going to write anything, it should be more than a book. It should be an ordeal.

Normally, I don't even think of the Oysters from May through August. I just luxuriate in the long hours of daylight; I take my morning coffee sitting out in the yard, I eat my lunch at the picnic table, and I often grill my supper over flaming chunks of my own chokecherry branches, the ones brought down by the winter's snow load. There's always plenty of spring cleanup work to do and chores like trimming the eight-foot Siberian pea hedge. So why did I sit around worrying about writing a mystery novel? I could start it in the fall. Or I could just call the whole thing off. I suppose it was a matter of pride, or face. I stubbornly refused to abandon the book, but it was ruining my summer.

I'd been a reader of mysteries all my life, beginning with Wilkie Collin's *The Woman in White* when I was a girl. But I was just a reader; I didn't analyze them. I certainly hadn't the foggiest idea of how to write one. I thought about some of my favorites.

Josephine Tey's *The Daughter of Time* opens with detective Alan Grant lying in a hospital bed, recuperating from injuries received from falling through a trapdoor while chasing a felon. Knowing he is fascinated by faces, a friend brings him an old portrait to analyze. Grant immediately decides this is the face of a sensitive, intelligent man, but the portrait is revealed to be Richard III, one of history's great villains. Banking more on his own skill in reading faces than on the reliability of historians, from his hospital bed Grant challenges history and finds—well, I won't spoil the book for anyone who hasn't read it. This particular approach involves digging into history, which is a possibility for me; I'd enjoy that. But what history?

The Napoleon Bonaparte books by Arthur Upfield are also favorites of mine. Bony, as the Australian detective prefers to be addressed, is half-aboriginal, college educated, and as sharp as any sleuth in fiction. He solves crimes all over the Australian subcontinent, in habitats so unfriendly and overpowering that they are as crucial to the story as are the murderer, the victim, and the detective. Perhaps I could use this interior Alaska subarctic location; it's one of the coldest places on the planet and could be an important part of my book. Besides, it's what I know; I live here.

As I went about my spring chores, picking up the winter's detritus of bottles, cans, and papers or planting and pruning and mulching, I pondered how I might begin. One day toward the end of May while I was taking a pickup load of trash to the dump—many Alaskan women own pickups; they are the most liberating thing since the pill—I got a bright idea. I would see if the library had any instruction books on how to write a mystery novel. I dropped off the load and sped back to the library to begin the search.

We have a beautiful library, a product of our Alaska oil money. Spacious, tastefully tiled and carpeted, it has some tall birch trees growing in the foyer. I've always loved this building but never so much as now. In five minutes I found a volume entitled *Detective Fiction: A Collection of Critical Essays*, edited by Robin W. Winks. I was relieved to discover how very simple writing a detective novel would be. According to W. H. Auden, in an essay entitled "The Guilty Vicarage," I would need

1.   a setting, an Eden-like Great Good Place;
2.   a closed society, closed so that the murderer and the victim belong to the same group;
3.   a victim, whose death casts a suspicion on everyone in the group;

4.   a murderer, a person who refuses to suffer and who claims the right to extinguish a life in order to make his or her life more bearable; and last,

5.   a detective.

The author observes further: "The corpse must shock not only because it is a corpse, but also because, even for a corpse, it is shockingly out of place, as when a dog makes a mess on a drawing room carpet."

With that under my hat I was ready to begin. But what Eden-like Great Good Place? After living in Alaska for more than forty years I hardly remembered what it was like living Outside, or in the Lower 48, as we say since we achieved statehood. So my Eden-like Great Good Place would have to be Fairbanks, Alaska.

What about the closed society? All of the organizations of which I was a member posed some problems. I'm sure the Unitarians wouldn't care to see their counterparts murdering or being murdered; neither would the League of Women Voters, nor the Retired Teachers, nor the American Association of University Women. Although, come to think of it, the Unitarians might enjoy it. They're famous for being able to laugh at themselves, and they relish being picked on by a certain radio humorist. They have even published a whole book of Unitarian jokes, like

Minister: Mary, is this a good time to talk about whether you'd prefer to be buried or cremated?

Mary: Surprise me.

Or:

I don't care who your father is, you can't walk on water while I'm fishing.

I won't rule out the Unitarians.

What about the victim? I mentally inventoried friends, relations, and a few prominent Fairbanksans, but with the exception of a politician or two, I couldn't think of a single person I would murder, even in fun. Then, while I was pruning my Siberian pea hedge the next day, the paper girl made her daily call, and I got my second bright idea: the *Daily Sourdough*.

I climbed down from the back of my pickup—I trim the hedge standing in the pickup box because the hedge is very high and deep and because the truck is easier to move, and more stable, than a ladder. Also, I'm less likely to fall out of the pickup box into the hedge, which is hard to get out of.

I showered, changed clothes, and jogged over the Cushman Street bridge to the *Daily Sourdough* building. The *Daily Sourdough* operation was not what I expected. Instead of being handed a pile of old newspapers, I was directed to a young woman at a computer who, I was told, researched anything needed by the staff; in fact, a young reporter was picking up some papers as I walked in. Abandoning the usual reticence of an unpublished writer, I explained to the young woman, and unintentionally to everyone within hearing range, that I was writing a murder mystery and I needed a list of murders that had taken place in Fairbanks during the last four years. I amended "murders" to "unnatural deaths." She said that ordinarily she would refer me to the Noel Wien Library, but since the *Daily Sourdough* kept just such a list for its own use, she would be glad to oblige.

She turned to the computer, fingered the keys, and out came two printed sheets of paper. I scanned them quickly, thanked her, and after noting the amused smile of the young reporter, I jogged home, where, after a cup of coffee, I looked over the list.

There were several spouse murders. In Anchorage they call them "Spenard divorces," because in earlier days, an inordinate number of people in that part of town found it handier to shoot or otherwise dispose of their unwanted mates rather than suffer the inconvenience of a divorce. I remembered a case where a husband pulled out a pistol and handed it to his wife, saying, "Go ahead, shoot me." She took it and plugged him right between the eyes.

"I didn't know I was such a good shot," she explained to the police, which is probably why she later claimed the death was accidental. Nowadays, I'm happy to say, Anchorage is a modern, civilized city, and spouse murders are frowned upon. They often draw a stiff prison sentence but not as stiff as for killing a female moose outside hunting season.

These were some of the unnatural deaths occurring in or around Fairbanks during the last four years:

1. Two young men were killed by gunshots, drug related.
2. A car bombing killed one man.
3. A depressed man shot his wife, then himself.
4. An elderly Native man froze to death in a snowbank.
5. A man shot and killed his mother-in-law, who wouldn't tell him where his wife was, and then killed himself.
6. A University of Alaska freshman was found dead in his car, an apparent suicide by carbon monoxide poisoning.
7. A crazed man shot and killed eight residents of a nearby village.
8. A construction worker was found stabbed to death in his hotel room, his bankroll missing.
9. A prostitute shot her pimp for refusing to sleep with her.
10. The body of a young woman, long missing, was found in a gravel pit.
11. A University of Alaska freshman, injured on the university ski trail, froze to death.
12. An elderly woman got out of her son's car to use the washroom at an out-of-town gas station, and was never seen again.
13. A trailer-house burned down in minus forty-degree weather: two people died.
14. A young woman disappeared, and was found raped and murdered.
15. The body of a missing University of Alaska freshman was found encased in ice on the banks of the Chena River during spring breakup.

And there were more, many more, but I had to stop. While I am as accustomed as anyone to reading about deaths in the daily newspaper, seeing four years' worth of accidents and murders compressed onto two pages made me feel that my Great Good Place, my Eden-like home, was very violent indeed. Especially when so many of the dead were young people; three were college students.

Alaska has the youngest population of the fifty states. I suppose that could be one reason why so many Alaskans die young. Young people seem drawn here by some Alaska mystique: they have a hunger for a far-off place, for the danger of braving an extreme climate, for the challenge of the difficult weather and terrain. They come to earn money for college or to get rich on construction jobs. Sometimes they fatally underestimate their experience and qualifications. Nor are older Alaskans immune. Seasoned sourdoughs die in small planes, in riverboats, on snowmachines. Tractors roll over; fishing boats sink. Even a simple cross-country hike can turn into tragedy if the hiker is alone and tries to ford an unfamiliar river or meets a cranky bear.

I decided to take a long, hot soak in the tub, my usual therapy when I feel depressed. I switched off the phone and soaked for about an hour. Then I went to bed.

Chapter 3

If you didn't make your troubles so amusing, you'd get more sympathy.

I didn't sleep well. I spent the night half-awake, brooding about all those dead people on the *Sourdough* list. So many of them were young people. I was jarred out of my reverie by the sound of someone pounding on my front door: it proved to be Andrew, my ten-year-old grandson, who grumped that he had been trying to phone me all morning. As usual, I had forgotten to switch on the phone after my bath the night before.

Andrew said the Chena River was clear of spring ice, so he and his friend CJ wanted to celebrate with a canoe trip. Andrew's parents were busy, so were CJ's. Would I accept an invitation to a peaceful afternoon on the river? The answer was not an automatic yes, since time and bitter experience had taught me to exercise a certain degree of caution before accepting my grandson's invitations. Time spent with Andrew is rarely peaceful, but with the exception of being cut in two by a speeding riverboat, what could happen? We were all experienced paddlers; I've been canoeing with Andrew since he was six. So, with my usual optimism, and because I could use the time on the river to do some serious thinking, I accepted. I had a feeling that my subconscious mind had been working feverishly all night and that something decisive had happened. I filled a thermos with hot cocoa, threw on some warm clothing, and we headed out.

The two boys donned lifejackets, hoisted my aluminum canoe to their shoulders, and began the three-block walk to the river. Popsie, my elderly poodle, and I followed with the paddles and the boys' idea of a light repast: a six-pack of pop, several kinds of chips and cookies, assorted candy bars, apples, and my cocoa. CJ was in the prow and Andrew was steersman as we set out. Lounging comfortably amidships with Popsie, I felt like Cleopatra in all her glory.

The trip was very pleasant. Canoes were out en masse; happily, there were not quite as many wake-raising riverboats. Conversation was minimal since the boys' mouths were full most of the time. We inspected beaver lodges, and we made an exploratory trip into Noyes Slough, a quiet backwater where waterfowl nest. Then, back on the river, we rejoined the throng of celebrating canoers and kayakers.

Sometime during the afternoon I realized that I had found my victim, or victims: the three college students who came to Alaska seeking adventure and who found death instead.

I suppose it was inevitable that a list of unnatural deaths would contain many young people. They have such a sense of their own immortality. In Fairbanks, high school students wear tennis shoes to school, and everywhere else, in minus-fifty-degree weather. They don't bother with hats, gloves, or scarves, and their parkas are often unzipped. Strangely, there is no noticeable occurrence of missing fingers, ears, or noses in their age group.

I was musing about how to proceed with my chosen victims when CJ gave a shout. We were drawing close to the Pump House Restaurant dock, our destination, which was already occupied by the sternwheeler *Discovery III*. The Pump House is an old, nicely restored building that once housed the pumps that supplied river water to several local gold mines. The *Discovery III*, an old-fashioned-looking vessel that plies the Chena and Tanana rivers twice daily in summer, looked packed to the gunwales. Some celebrity must have been on board, as well as several hundred tourists, a news reporter, a photographer, and unfortunately, Andrew and CJ's friend, Buzzie. The boys shouted greetings back and forth, then Andrew stood up, waved his paddle, and over we went.

Being safely lifejacketed, we were in no danger. My heart managed to withstand the sudden plunge into the forty-eight-degree water. We scrambled onto the upturned canoe and in less than five minutes we were rescued by two men who had been dining on the Pump House deck. They simply started their riverboat, which was tied at the Pump House dock, and hauled us out of the water, but not before the reporter on the *Discovery III* recognized the "writer" he had seen the day before at the *Daily Sourdough,* researching murder, and not before the photographer got a shot of me astride the canoe, a dripping poodle in my arms and a grinning ten-year-old on either side.

We made the front page of the Sunday edition of the *Sourdough:* a huge photograph above the fold with the caption "First Dip of the Season." I was identified as the "well-known Fairbanks writer," currently working on a mystery novel. The damned phone almost rang off the hook. Everyone I knew in town inquired solicitously about my health, but I knew they were having a good laugh.

Several of the Oysters asked if I had started my mystery novel, a logical question after the *Sourdough* gaffe. I didn't say much, only that I thought I had found my victims, three college students, and that I was going to change their deaths from suicide and accident to murder.

As I look back I keep seeing places where things might have been different if only I hadn't talked so much; but now, with twenty-twenty hindsight, I have to absolve myself of any responsibility for what happened. Even if I'd never said a word about what I was going to write, the outcome would have been the same. Much had already been done that couldn't be undone, and if I made mistakes, I've paid for them.

But on that Sunday, I was looking only forward. I decided to go down to my cabin at Birch Lake to lick my wounds, and I resisted the urge to borrow Andrew. I just threw some food in a bag and left.

❄ ❄ ❄ ❄ ❄ ❄

My hopes for a few days' solitude at the cabin were soon dashed; I had just made a nice fire by the lake to grill some sausages when I heard a car coming up the hill. Marcia Wayman and Katie George joined me at the fire. Marcia refused the sausages, but Katie had one, with a beer.

"We were worried about you," said Katie, between bites. "We didn't think you should go off alone, after being…almost drowned…in that icy river."

There was laughter in Katie's eyes despite the sympathetic tone. Eventually the talk got around to my book. Marcia asked such probing questions I began to think she was a closet whodunit reader. I decided not to give away the plot—actually I didn't have any plot. I just mentioned that I had decided to use the three students as my victims. By the first meeting of the Oysters, in late September, I said, I should have several chapters written. There'd be some answers then.

The mosquitoes were pretty bad, even with the fire, so my guests didn't stay long. I escaped into the cabin and studied the *Sourdough* list of Fairbanks deaths. Why couldn't I take the information about the dead students straight from the *Sourdough* stories, change names and biographical details, and weave some fictional web to explain their deaths? I could have the boys die at the hands of an imaginary murderer who had some obscure motive for wanting them dead. The difficult part would be finding that motive and developing some kind of relationship among the boys.

Despite distracting visits from several more Oysters—Florence Hokkainen and Abbie Buffmire also showed up—I continued to concentrate on my mystery. I had my geographical locale, interior Alaska; my Great Good Place, Fairbanks; and my victims, the three college boys. All I needed now was the "closed society," which should include the victims, the suspects, and of course, the murderer, who would also be one of the suspects. I mustn't forget the detective, who would be, more or less, me. I seemed to fit the description perfectly. According to W. H. Auden's "The Guilty Vicarage,"

> The amateur detective genius may have weaknesses to give him aesthetic interest, but they must not be of the kind which outrage ethics. The most satisfactory weaknesses are the solitary vices of eating and drinking or childish

boasting. In his sexual life, the detective must be either celibate or happily married.

The description fit me perfectly.

I stayed at the lake three days. I fished—three trout and one landlocked salmon—hiked, and worked on the grounds. As I cut and stacked wood, I thought about my book and planned strategies. I would have to go to the library in the morning and begin research on the first student to die, the boy who took his own life.

I closed the cabin and drove the sixty miles home. Next morning I threw on some clothes, ate a bowl of oatmeal, and was about to step out the door when I remembered that the library didn't open until ten o'clock. Damn! I cleaned the kitchen, unloaded the car, threw a load of laundry into the washing machine, and then walked to the library, where I was waiting at the doors when they opened.

Chapter 4

When did the Great Anxiety begin?

The first student to die was Mark Sandberg, who reportedly committed suicide by carbon monoxide poisoning in his little two-seater automobile on November 16, 1989. He'd left the dormitory late that afternoon, ostensibly to see someone about part-time work, and never returned to his room. He was found about ten p.m. parked in front of the country club on Yankovich Road, directly behind the university. Some boys on snowmobiles had thought at first that he was sleeping and then decided that it was unlikely at minus thirty degrees, especially since his car wasn't running. His little car must have run until it was out of gas, which probably wasn't long, as most teenagers run their cars on empty.

Retired Air Force Colonel Eric Sandberg and his wife wouldn't believe that their son had taken his own life; they insisted there must have been some kind of foul play. Mark had written and called home regularly. Just the day before his death they'd had a long telephone conversation with him; he'd asked his parents if they would spring for some new skis for Christmas, and they'd said yes. He'd been in excellent spirits, excited about being in Alaska, the state of his birth. He liked all his classes and was planning to return home to Santa Barbara over Christmas break. Mark had always been outgoing and well adjusted, they said. They'd noticed no change in him in the weeks before his death.

Mark had been an outstanding student and athlete in high school. Tall, blond, and good-looking, he was well liked by his contemporaries and his teachers alike. He was outgoing, friendly, a communicator, not a boy to sit around brooding. Why would such a boy commit suicide, his parents wanted to know. But no one had any answers, and so the sorrowing parents, with their sixteen-year-old daughter, Sonja, claimed the remains of their son and brother and went back to California.

The police had questioned everyone who knew Mark. Had he ever seemed homesick? Had he talked a lot about his parents? His sister? But no one could recall his expressing anything but joy on being able to return to Alaska and delight at the challenges it presented. Friends and instructors all were shocked by his inexplicable act. The coroner's jury delivered a verdict of "suicide while of unsound mind," and the life and death of this boy soon faded from Alaska memory.

I felt as sad as if I had known him and I began to wish that I had chosen some other victims. Why *had* I chosen him and the others? It wasn't consciously done; there was something about the incongruity, the very unlikelihood that three university freshmen during that short span of eighteen months would die sudden deaths.

I couldn't get that boy out of my mind. I dreamed about him all night, and waking logy and depressed, I pondered the strangeness of his death. Everyone said he was a loving son and brother; why hadn't he left a note for his parents and Sonja? Perhaps a sudden fit of depression? But no one interviewed could remember ever seeing him the least bit depressed. I needed to know more about suicide. I made a note to do some research.

Outside the house the day was sunny, warm, and inviting. In my yard chokecherries were in full bloom, and the lilacs soon would be. My favorite time of the year, and I moped indoors. The ringing of the phone jarred me out of my reverie. I didn't want to talk to anyone. It kept on ringing. It had to be my grandson, Andrew, who never gives up. I dragged myself over to answer it.

Andrew wanted me to take him and his friend CJ to the movies. I had no trouble saying no. Several months ago he had talked me into renting a film called *The Gang Who Couldn't Shoot Straight*. From his description, it sounded like a great comedy for kids. I rented it and agreed to let Andrew and several friends view it at my house on a Sunday afternoon. I started it for them and went into the kitchen to fix some snacks.

When I returned with a tray I couldn't believe my eyes or ears. I immediately packed up film, Andrew, CJ, Buzzie, and Greaser and dumped them at their front doors.

"Andrew," I said, "I'm not having anything to do with you and movies ever again. I remember how you conned me into renting that last one; the language you picked up from it was bad enough, but did you have to use it right in front of your parents?"

"Aw, come on, Gram, all I said was 'blow it out your...'"

"I know what you said, and I know what your mother thinks of me, too."

"She didn't blame you, Gram, honest. I heard her tell Dad you weren't responsible, and that I was just like you. I swear. She likes you a lot."

"I believe you. I'm sure that's just what she said. And now, Andrew, for once, you are not going to involve me in one of your nefarious schemes. Goodbye." I had forgiven him long enough to go on a canoe trip, and where did it get me? In the river.

At least he had raised my blood pressure a little. I struggled into some clothes and dragged myself to the library.

Jason Calloway's body was found just off the university cross-country ski trail, covered with snow. An accomplished skier, he had apparently rounded a blind curve at a fast clip and for some reason had left the trail and crashed into a large birch tree, knocking himself out. He had actually frozen to death. There were several bruises on his head and some skin left on the tree trunk where his head had struck.

Jason had left his dorm late the previous afternoon and was found the following morning by an alert skier who'd spotted a solitary ski sticking up among the scrubby birches along the trail. A light snowfall during the night had completely covered his body. The skier, himself a student, uncovered enough to determine that the victim was dead and then skied back to the university for help.

Jason was born while his father, a major in the Air Force, was stationed in Alaska. According to the *Sourdough*, the boy had been an outstanding student and athlete. Another one! He'd had a strong predilection for science and had received several local and national science awards at his high-school graduation. He'd turned down a full scholarship to Princeton in order to enter the University of Alaska. An only child, he was described as tall, with fair hair and blue eyes.

After the coroner's jury delivered a verdict of accidental death, his parents accompanied his body back to Seattle. There was a picture from the *Sourdough* of a tall officer and his wife being seen off at the airport by a delegation of Jason's friends. His death didn't get as much news coverage as Mark Sandberg's had, probably because there never seemed to be any mystery about how he died.

I completed my notes and just sat there, thinking. Somehow, when I started this project, I hadn't expected to be involved in so much death. I had been reading mysteries for forty years, and mysteries are all about death, but I wasn't prepared. Already the deaths of two boys were more than I seemed able to handle.

Chapter 5

But it's not the poet's fault if the world won't give
him peace enough to write poetry?

Most Alaskans are a satisfied, even smug lot. The reasons are not hard to find. We live in breathtakingly beautiful surroundings. I don't mean downtown Fairbanks; I mean the wooded hills that surround the Tanana Valley; the rugged mountain ranges, snowcapped even in summer, massive and overpowering when one is among them and ghostly and haunting from a distance. I think it is fair to say that on a clear day, one is never out of sight of some mountain range.

Then there is size. Only by flying over or around the state can you get an idea of the vastness of Alaska. There are many places I have not yet visited, since flying is expensive and Alaska has very few roads. Writer John McPhee said, in *Coming into the Country*, that Alaska has two roads: one goes from Anchorage to Fairbanks, and the other from Fairbanks to Anchorage.

Living in Fairbanks in winter is like living on an island: in the extreme cold only the young, the intrepid, and the foolish drive more than a few miles from home, and then only with great care. We don't casually drive to the next town for dinner or a movie; there is no next town, there is only Nenana, a village of several hundred people, sixty miles away.

From March through October we can drive to Anchorage, 370 miles south, with only an occasional snowfall in the mountain passes to trouble us. We drive south to Chitina (pronounced Chit-na) or Valdez (Val-deez) to fish for salmon, and we explore our fifteen thousand miles of roads. The rest of the time we spend isolated in this little anthill in the wilderness, except for periodic escapes to Hawaii or Mexico to thaw out.

But the cold and dark and isolation are only one part of the difficulty of living in Alaska. The other part concerns family. Unless you are a remittance person and paid by your family to stay in Alaska, or unless you are a native of Alaska and have your entire family living here, the distance that separates grown children from aging parents, and grandchildren from grandparents and aunts and uncles and cousins can seem unendurable. We spend an inordinate amount of time and money traipsing back and forth across the continent trying to remedy this situation, but there is no satisfactory remedy.

When a family like mine consists of two aging parents in Vermont and a single living child in Alaska, five thousand miles away, the problem can become acute. My problem started five years ago when my father looked at my mother blankly one morning and asked her who she was and what she was doing in his house. Nothing my startled mother could say would convince him that she was his wife, that she was not some interloper trying to steal his money and break up his marriage. He refused to sleep in the same bed with her any longer.

"I never played my wife false, and I'm not going to start now," he said, and he called her a harlot for wanting to sleep with a married man. He finally agreed to accept her as his hired girl. He was then seventy-eight and she was seventy-four. The obvious solution would seem that they should go into a retirement home, or move in with me, but they didn't want to give up their big house in Vermont or move to Alaska, or anywhere in between, and I wasn't willing to give up my home, either.

My mother was alternately angry and depressed about her husband's mental condition, not that she hadn't developed some little quirks of her own. She insisted on placing scraps of food on their patio every night because she liked to watch the grateful skunks, raccoons, possums, foxes, stray cats, and dogs through the glass door.

They became regular visitors, and as their numbers multiplied, the patio got to be more and more of a mess. And in summer the varmints raided my father's garden, especially his corn.

There were other difficulties, like the issue of my father's driving. A certain amount of driving was necessary, if they were to stay in their own home. Mother hadn't driven in years, and Father shouldn't be driving either, Mother said. He couldn't tell a truck from a cow in the middle of the road. I suggested she ask his doctor to call him in for a check-up, including an eye exam, followed by a driving test. She did. He passed both. I suspect that because Vermont has such a large elderly population, Father is just not at the bottom of the driving curve.

A friend of Mother's, who is in her nineties, frequently drives the sixteen-mile round trip from St. Albans to take Mother out to dinner and a show or to their women's club meetings. Father, of course, wouldn't be seen in public with the "hired girl."

I really didn't think the two should be living on their own any longer, but several years ago they'd inveigled a promise from me that I would never place them in a retirement home against their wishes. Nor would they allow me to hire a full-time housekeeper. Meanwhile, they took turns phoning me, each to complain about the outrageous behavior of the other.

Bearing the fruits of my research, I trudged home from the library. As I entered the house the phone was ringing. It was my father, complaining that the previous night one of those varmints "the girl" insisted on feeding on the terrace, a skunk, had given him a good spraying while he, Father, was taking a little midnight stroll. He'd had to strip down, buck naked was how he expressed it, only to find the girl had locked him out of the house. Dressed in gunny sacks from the barn and reeking, he'd roused some neighbors who finally reached Mother on the telephone. When she let him in he'd fired her on the spot, but she, quite naturally, wouldn't leave. He wanted to hire another girl, one who would know her place. If I didn't come out there right now he wouldn't answer for what might happen.

I told him I couldn't possibly leave until August (when it rains every day); he would just have to hang on a bit longer. We had a long and difficult conversation. I couldn't reason with him, but at last he agreed to postpone any further action regarding "the girl" until my visit in August.

Father must have sat down and promptly fallen asleep, because fifteen minutes later my mother phoned. She didn't mention skunks; she just complained that my father was hoarding his retirement checks in his desk drawer and she couldn't pay their bills. I told her to take the checks while he was sleeping, deposit them by mail, and arrange for future checks to be direct-deposited into their account. I also suggested she start phasing out her nocturnal visitors, but she said that was not an option. If my father would stop wandering around the yard at all hours of the night, nothing would happen. I told her, like Father, to hang on for a few more weeks.

Their longtime neighbors had been replaced by younger families, who kindly made themselves available when the old couple needed help. The old couple, however, wouldn't ask for help from anyone but me. I telephoned the nearest neighbors and told them I would be there soon and hired one of their teenagers to check on my parents twice daily and to run errands, if needed. At the moment any real solution to their problems was beyond me.

I sat down in the living room, depressed about my parents. Coffee and a tuna sandwich helped raise my spirits and fueled the walk back to the library.

The third student, William de Forest Hodgson, had disappeared on April 7, 1990. His body was found four weeks later on the banks of the Chena River, near Alaskaland, our pioneer theme park. Encased in a shroud of ice, the boy's body had apparently floated from some- place upstream.

William . . . Bill . . . had entered the university at midterm, in January. His father, Brig. General David H. Hodgson, was retiring from the Air Force, and Bill had delayed his entrance into college so he could help his parents make the move from England to their new home in San Antonio, Texas. Another military family! Was this nor- mal for Alaska, with its many military bases? I made a note.

Like the other two boys, Bill was an outstanding student. He'd been offered full scholarships from both Brown and Tufts, but he would have neither; he wanted only to return to Alaska, the state of his birth. During his short stay at the University of Alaska his grades were straight *A*s, and although he'd enrolled too late to make the basketball team, he'd been practicing with them and probably would have made the team the following year.

When Bill disappeared, his parents had flown up from Texas to take charge of the search. They'd appeared on television, appealing for information; there had been several articles in the *Sourdough*, and later paid ads that included photographs, descriptions, and offers of a reward. After three weeks the grieving parents had flown back to Texas. A week later Bill's body was found on the riverbank. The parents returned.

The picture in the *Sourdough* was of a tall, handsome boy, described as blond, blue-eyed, five foot eleven, 155 pounds. The *Sourdough* hadn't printed pictures of the other two boys. The coroner's verdict was, once more, accidental death.

I took my notes and went home. I wanted to go over the information about each boy and see what I could do to connect them in some way, to make their deaths at the hand of a single killer feasible. But first I had to take Popsie for a walk and dig something out of the freezer for my dinner. I found myself begrudging time spent on mundane things like housework, walking dogs, even eating and sleeping. My yard was a mess. As I set out with Popsie I looked over my lawn, which badly needed a trim. My neighbor, Dennis Wheeler, chose that moment to walk over for a chat. Dennis, one of several African-American members of our police department, is tall, handsome, very muscular, and very nice. He stood beside me, studying the scene of neglect.

"I've been meaning to come over to see you, Heather. Been sick or something?"

"No, just busy. You don't look too sharp yourself. How's Raysheen?" His wife is on the police force too.

"She's fine." He studied the thriving crop of dandelions. "She just made sergeant."

Uh oh! She's caught up with him!

"Like me to cut the grass? If it gets much taller you'll need a scythe."

"I can do it. It takes only a few minutes with my lawn tractor." I suspected that Dennis's nose was a bit out of joint that his rookie wife had overtaken him so quickly. The presence of two police persons on the adjoining property contributes much to my feeling of security. Dennis bought the house four years ago and lived there alone for two years. When a beautiful, tall, long-legged black rookie joined the police force, he immediately offered to help her sharpen her Tai Kwon Do, Jujitsu, and other martial arts skills. He was crippled for two weeks afterwards. Undaunted, he continued to court the lady, and a year ago they were married. Dennis, who is the chief cook in their household, brings me lots of goodies from his kitchen. Raysheen too drops in for periodic chats.

All of a sudden I had one of those flashes of intuition that had marked this project from the beginning.

"Dennis," I asked, trying to conceal my eagerness, "I'm writing a book about the deaths of three university students. Is there any chance that I could see their official files?"

He stood there stroking his chin as he considered my request. I could almost read his mind: harmless old dame, no trouble to the police, no accidents, no drinking, no drugs, police never called to the house, no trouble of any kind. Not realizing that all of the above statements were soon to become inoperative, he decided to humor the old girl.

"Sure," he answered kindly, "why not? Give me some names and dates. I'll need a few days to dig them out. You can't take them home; you'll have to read them at headquarters. I'll let you know when they're ready."

I was so elated that I ran both Popsie and the lawn tractor at top speed within the hour. Then I broiled a steak, nuked a potato, and even tossed myself a double Manhattan. What a stroke of genius! What a windfall! Hallelujah!

One of my favorite first lines in literature is by P. G. Wodehouse. He said, "it's always when a fellow is feeling particularly braced with things in general that Fate sneaks up behind him with a bit of lead piping." Just as I was about to repair to the tub for some triumphant soaking, the phone rang. It was Lead Piping.

Chapter 6

Time is all that matters. There isn't as much of it as there used to be.

Lead Piping, otherwise known as Myra Goodman, was my college roommate. She and I have maintained a spotty correspondence over forty years and five thousand miles. As they were preparing to leave for Japan, her husband, Marvin, a retired professor of geology, suddenly got the idea that they should take a few days' layover in Alaska. Could I put them up? Better yet, could I take a few days off and drive with them around the state? Marvin was working on a geology textbook, and Alaska is well known to be rich in interesting geological sites.

People are always asking me if I can "take some time off" to do something or other. The request is usually accompanied by a smile, the implication being that I'm always "off," that I am on one perpetual vacation. It's just not so. Most retired people I know work very hard. Damn! Why did I ever think I could get away with starting a serious project like a book during the summer? As if there weren't enough to do working around the house and grounds, gardening, pruning, getting ready for winter. We're always getting ready for winter.

Then there's the matter of guests. Everyone wants to visit Alaska, and I never minded before. But this time I minded very much, though I couldn't bring myself to say, "No, Myra, I can't do it." They would be here in three days. They would stay for four.

The house was grubby; so was I. I looked about the way the lawn had before I cut it yesterday. There was practically no food in the house, and the car would have to be serviced. Damn again! I put my notes away. God only knew when I would get back to them. I made my list, I made appointments, and three days later I was ready and waiting at the airport when Myra and Marvin debarked.

We allowed one day for them to see Fairbanks and environs. That meant a visit to the university museum, with its displays of prehistoric animals. My favorites are the huge wooly mammoth, the blue steppe bison, and the mastodon tusks. There are also many fine displays of Eskimo and Indian costumes, fishing and hunting equipment of all sorts, and crafts, like beadwork and ivory carving.

We visited the Georgeson Botanical Garden, with its fine displays of flowers and vegetables that thrive in this subarctic region. We spent an afternoon on the sternwheeler *Discovery III*, which took us to a fish camp on the Tanana River, with its working fish wheel and drying racks. We had dinner at the outdoor Salmon Bake, in Alaskaland, and an evening at the Malemute Saloon in the mining village of Ester. Nor did we overlook the Trans-Alaska Pipeline, a few miles north of town. At the end of the day I was bushed, but they were still raring to go. The morning of the second day we took off for Denali Park and Preserve, and Mount McKinley, which most Alaskans prefer to call by its Athabascan name, *Denali*, The Great One.

Well, I didn't know it, but we were setting out on the definitive geological expedition of the century. Twenty-five miles out, Marvin got a headache. Myra said he always got a headache if he wasn't in the driver's seat. Naturally, I removed myself and scuttled my plan of rotating the driving. Marvin took control of the steering wheel and didn't relinquish it for the remainder of the trip. Popsie and I were relegated permanently to the back seat. I think I behaved rather well: rather than ruin the trip, I decided to be a damned good sport, and that's what I was.

Marvin had brought photographic equipment to record the innumerable examples of geological structures for his textbook. Every stop was accompanied by a—rather good, I must admit—lecture on the "world class" glaciers, the braiding of streams, and the layering visible on the mountain sides. He pointed out evidence of some ancient inland sea and many other geological phenomena. At least somebody's book was getting written.

At Denali National Park we camped overnight. Myra and Marvin had brought sleeping bags and a tent; Popsie and I slept in the back of my station wagon. I awoke in the morning after the best sleep I'd had in days, if not weeks. Marvin, the first to wake, had made a fire in the grill, and the friendly aroma of coffee and bacon permeated the area. I forgave him everything. I hadn't dreamed of dead boys, nor had I thought of them once since leaving home.

We took the early morning bus tour, the only way to see the park since cars are not allowed. It was a charmed trip; we saw a record number of bears, moose, caribou, a mother fox with three kits, and many ptarmigan and spruce hens. The bus driver made frequent stops, so everyone was able to take as many pictures as he or she wished, especially of The Mountain, Denali.

I recommended that we bypass Anchorage, it being much like stateside cities of similar size. We Fairbanksans say that the best thing about Anchorage is that it's only fifty (air) minutes from Alaska (Fairbanks). On the other hand, in Anchorage they consider Fairbanks "the bush." We continued as far as Palmer and camped that night at the great Matanuska glacier. Around the campfire, as we ate our grilled sausages, Marvin told us how anything that falls into the glacier is slowly ripped apart by its grinding action as the ice moves forward. Sometimes the glacier spews out paleoanthropological treasures, like corpses of perfectly preserved humans and animals, which were somehow bypassed by the grinding action.

Next morning we made the run to Fairbanks by way of the old Glenn Highway and the old Anchorage–Fairbanks highway, the Richardson, which, being somewhat longer and rougher, has less traffic than the newer Parks Highway. My guests easily caught their seven p.m. flight for Anchorage and Japan. Despite having been a grudging hostess, I really had enjoyed the trip, but I was ready for them to go. I saw them to their plane and went home, physically exhausted but mentally restored and impatient to resume my writing project.

Chapter 7

Like a minor poet (which in my high moments I am)
I was outraged by the paradoxes of mortality.

The house felt strangely empty. Odd, as Myra and Marvin hadn't really spent very much time in it. I put away the camping gear, cleaned out the food box, and disposed of the dirty clothes. I felt like sitting right down and working on my book, but what could I do? Then I thought of Dennis Wheeler. Maybe he'd made arrangements for me to have access to the boys' official files.

I trotted the short distance to his house, but dammit, he wasn't there. His house was locked up tight and his motor home was missing. He and Raysheen had probably gone to Valdez or Chitina for some king salmon fishing. I glumly climbed into a steaming tub and soaked off the accumulated grime from the trip. Then, worn out from the long day, the long trip, and the long stretch of being on my best behavior, I fell into bed and slept soundly and long.

It's a funny thing how most Alaskans can sleep through the long daylight hours of summer. When I first came to the north I had to darken my bedroom with black shades, because the twilight at midnight and broad daylight at three in the morning were difficult for a cheechako, that is, a newcomer, to get used to. Now I'm hardly aware of the nocturnal daylight, and it certainly has no effect on my sleeping.

I could have used soundproofing, then, too. In those days Fairbanksans used to work around the clock, running their chain saws, lawn mowers, sanders, and working on their pickup trucks any hour of the day or night. There were as many people on the streets at night as there were during the day. Neighbors carried on conversations outside your bedroom window at three in the morning. Neighborhood children seemed to stay up all night, too, playing games in the street. There was a curfew for children then, but it had no noticeable effect. Now, most of us round up the kids at a decent hour and try to remember not to use noisy equipment when our neighbors want to sleep. If we forget, our neighbors are likely to remind us.

I awoke early next morning raring to go. Even before I made coffee I ran over to Dennis Wheeler's house to see if he had come in during the night, but no luck. I cooked the last of the bacon and eggs from the trip, then I read through my notes and came across a reminder to look into the matter of suicide. Perfect. That would be my assignment for the day.

The library had a number of books on suicide. I thumbed through several and finally selected *The Savage God: A Study of Suicide,* by A. Alvarez, and *The Myth of Sisyphus,* by Albert Camus. I checked them out and headed home. Once there I eyed all the mail and newspapers that had built up during my trip, neatly boxed by Andrew, and decided that the books took precedence.

By lunchtime I had a lot of notes. Alvarez, in *The Savage God,* called on a number of other authors: I learned that "suicide often seems…to be performed…most unaccountably…in the very bosom of happiness" [a quote Alvarez attributed to Montesquieu].

> It goes without saying that external misery has little to do with suicide. The figures are higher in the wealthy industrialized countries than in the underdeveloped, higher among the professional middle classes than among the poor.…
>
> Suicide is a confession of failure, of lives that no longer made sense.…
>
> Social isolation is a more powerful stimulus to self-destruction than…indigenous poverty.

... egoistic suicide occurs when the individual is not properly integrated into society, but is instead thrown onto his own resources.

For suicide to be recognized for what it is there must be an unequivocal note or a setting so unambiguous as to leave the survivors no alternatives.

Suicide may be a declaration of bankruptcy which passes judgment on a life as one long history of failures....75% of all suicides and would-be suicides give clear warning of their intentions beforehand.

And, said Camus in *The Myth of Sisyphus*, "suicide is prepared within the silence of the heart."

I was hungry and tired. I rummaged in the freezer until I found a package of frozen chili. That and a beer restored me somewhat. I skipped the mail and newspapers and picked up my morning's gleanings.

Mark did indeed appear to have died in the very bosom of happiness. And certainly he came from an affluent background. In no way could suicide have been a confession of failure; his life had been crowned with success after success from the start. Of course, only he knew whether his life made sense, but until the day of his death he seemed to know where he was going. And he was in no way socially isolated.

As for not being properly integrated into society, he had come to a strange, hostile environment, adjusted to college-level classes, made friends, participated in sports, and was about to add part-time work to his busy schedule. He seemed to have plenty of personal resources to draw on. He wasn't even included in the peak ages for suicide, which are, according to Alvarez, between twenty-five and forty-four and from fifty-five to sixty-five. No note was ever found, nor could anyone say that the setting for his death was "unambiguous." No wonder his parents wouldn't believe the coroner's verdict. But as for leaving the survivors no alternatives... what alternatives were there? A death "prepared within the silence of the heart"?

Chapter 8

Horror comes through, Felicity absents itself awhile.

After all that reading, I was no closer to understanding why Mark had taken his own life. How *could* he have done it? He was so well loved. Can anyone who is truly loved kill himself? Alvarez didn't say, nor did Camus.

The thought of that lovely boy going off to end his life, a life that should have been productive and happy, unsettled me. I didn't know what to do with myself. Even Popsie caught my depression and stayed discreetly in her basket. Finally, I resorted to my panacea-of-last-resort: when in doubt, make a mess. I decided to clean out the shed. It was jammed to the roof with all sorts of things intended to be recycled: bundles of newspapers, bags of glass bottles and jars, plastic milk containers, aluminum cans, rags. I could hardly move without tripping over something. I lifted out bag after bag, bundle after bundle, hardly knowing what I was doing.

As I lifted a large bundle of *Daily Sourdoughs*, the string broke and they scattered all over the place. I started to collect them, but instead found myself scanning headlines, and then stories. It seemed as if I had never seen some of them before.

An article about the annual report on unnatural deaths in Alaska caught my eye. I had often heard that we had an inordinately high suicide rate in Alaska, and there it was in black and white: ninety-five suicides last year, most of them young males between fourteen and forty-four. I've heard that other northern countries like Finland, Norway, Sweden, Russia, and Denmark have high suicide rates, but according to Alvarez, that is not so. Finland does have the second-highest suicide rate in the world, or at least it did, but the runners-up are not in Scandinavia, but in Central Europe: Hungary, Austria, and Czechoslovakia. In all of these countries, as in Alaska, alcohol consumption is a factor. Extremely long, cold, dark winters, isolation, and high alcohol consumption seem to go together.

Young Native Alaskan men, who find themselves caught between cultures, one very old and one very new, seem particularly vulnerable. In a time of diminishing resources and increasing regulations, they try to cling to their traditional hunting and fishing lifestyles, at the same time coveting the accoutrements of modern living that they see on their television sets. Some live in isolated villages that lack educational and job opportunities, but uprooting and moving to Fairbanks or Anchorage exacerbates the problem. Life for these young people on the cusp must seem alternately frustrating, lonely, and pointless.

Strangely, old sourdoughs in their seventies and eighties, after living long, active lives alone in their wilderness cabins, will occasionally end their lives, not in the fall, unable to face the prospect of one more desperately hard, lonely winter, but in the spring or early summer. When the world has turned green, when flowers are blooming, and birds singing, they put a bullet through their heads. There are one or two of these old sourdough suicides every year. Alvarez says that the cycle of self-destruction follows precisely that of nature: it declines in autumn, reaches its low in midwinter and then begins to rise slowly with the sap. Its climax is in early summer, May and June. In July it begins once more to drop.

Mark Sandberg had ostensibly taken his own life in November, a low point in the cycle of self-destruction, one more reason to doubt the verdict of the coroner's jury.

I decided to save that page since it seemed to bear out my contention that Alaskans die young. I was sitting on a milk crate musing about what I had just read when an auto horn blasted my reverie. I looked up to find Dennis and Raysheen Wheeler in their motor home, parked in my drive. I walked over to greet Raysheen. She was gorgeous, as usual, with that wondrous look of fragility that belied her ability to send overconfident males flying through the air. Dennis disappeared into the vehicle and quickly reappeared with a large, neatly wrapped parcel that could only be a king salmon.

"Twenty pounds. Think you can handle that?"

"You bet I can. Rowe and his gang will help." Then, hoping not to appear ungrateful, I blurted, "Dennis, about those police files, did you...?"

"Oh, sure. I tried to tell you, but you were never home. You can go anytime. Just mention my name and ask for the files. Look, we got our quota, got to get it in the freezer." And he drove off to attend to more important matters.

Happily hugging the big salmon, I went inside to stow it in the refrigerator. I thought better of it and stowed it in the freezer; I didn't have time for any family dinners just then.

When my son, Rowe, was a boy he and I used to take a tent and dip nets and drive the four hundred miles down to Chitina to get our own salmon. One year especially stands out. The salmon were swimming in from the Copper River to a pond by way of a shallow stream. One stretch of the stream was so shallow that the fish had to wiggle, totally exposed, over a muddy hump. Rowe and I threw down our nets and picked up sticks. We stunned the fish and then tossed them onto the bank. We had our quota in no time, and inasmuch as we were fishing for meat, not for sport, we were quite satisfied with our means of obtaining it. We'd probably end up in jail if we did that today. On the way home we'd stopped at a convenient glacier for ice.

I sat there reminiscing about old times for a few minutes, then roused myself and got back to work. I'd made quite a satisfactory mess of the shed. But I wasn't going to finish the job; that would have to wait until tomorrow. To tell the truth, I felt suddenly overwhelmed. All that business about suicide. Once again, I couldn't fathom how such a boy could have killed himself. It didn't make sense.

I suppose I was beginning to realize what I was letting myself in for at the police station. I was going to meet the three dead boys face to face. This project, until now, had had an aura of unreality about it.

It was still something I might yet escape, if I chose. How would I feel after tomorrow, when they became inescapably, irrevocably real?

I was at police headquarters by eight o'clock the next morning. The files were handed over to me without a word. I took them to a small conference room and opened the first one, Mark's.

Well, I had known it wouldn't be easy; in fact, I had expected it to be quite terrible. It was many times worse than that. There was a color picture of Mark as he was found sitting in his little car, slumped over the steering wheel. He might have been any weary teenager snatching a bit of rest after a night of partying. He was wearing a bright blue parka and red knitted ski hat.

The next picture, with the car door open, showed his feet, running shoes resting on the pedals; and the next was a shot of a rubber hose running from the exhaust pipe to the window opposite the driver's side, stuffed with insulation to prevent leakage. I turned the page again and there he lay on a slab in the morgue, still clothed in his outer gear. And in the next one—in the next one—his eyes were open... brilliant sky blue... staring at me.

What an ass. What an old fool. I sat there, tears running down my face. I clapped my hands over my mouth and just sat there until my sobs subsided. I swabbed my eyes and continued.

There was Mark, stripped of his down jacket, ski cap, shoes, and gloves. He lay there as if asleep, wearing a University of Alaska T-shirt and blue jeans. Mrs. Sandberg's pretty boy, with his red-gold hair, narrow arched nose, and strong cleft chin. He was long of limb and athletic looking, and I felt as if he could wake in the next instant and join his friends in a snowball fight.

The following pictures showed Mark with succeeding layers of clothing removed, until at last he lay there completely nude. The only mark on his entire body seemed to be the discolored bruise on his left forehead, from the steering wheel, the report said, but I noticed some small scratches on one shin that looked recent but completely healed. They were not mentioned in the report.

I made a few notes from the information on Mark's parents, but there was little that hadn't been mentioned in the newspapers. I went on to the next file. I sat there looking at it, dreading to open it yet knowing I had to. But I didn't have to. Who said I had to open that file? I could pick them all up and turn them in at the desk and never think about them again. Then I remembered Mark's blue eyes staring hypnotically into mine, and I opened the file, accidentally flipping it open to the middle.

I gasped in astonishment. The police must have mixed up the files, for there on the slab lay another Mark, with his bright-colored hair and blue eyes. I opened the first file again, Mark's file, to the shot of him with his eyes open, and held it next to the picture of Jason. There must be a mistake. It was another picture of Mark, blond and blue-eyed, only he was dressed differently. He was wearing a gray down jacket and a yellow Scandinavian knitted hat.

It wasn't Mark. Closer examination revealed a more oval-shaped face, more quizzical eyebrows, and fuller lips. I turned back a few pages. There was the ski trail. There was the snow-covered mound, just off the ski trail. There were the scrubby birches, one of which, on closer examination, revealed itself to be a cross-country ski. And there were three large birch trees, the one at the foot of the mound bearing the scar of the impact. It must have been a sharp-eyed student who recognized, in the half-light of a winter morning, that this was the scene of a lonely tragedy. It reminded me of a story I used to weep over as a child, about a small brother and sister who lost their way in the woods, and when they lay down to die, the birds covered them over with leaves. Only Jason was covered with snow.

The next picture showed Jason, snow brushed off. Like Mark, he appeared to be sleeping. And in the next one, there he was again, his eyes open. I opened the first file and lay the photo of Jason next to that of Mark. They might almost have been twins.

Well, they were clearly two different boys, but the color of the hair and skin were identical, and they were very like in their build, although Jason may have been a tad heavier. Mark's face was long and narrow, while Jason had a more oval face, with high cheekbones. But each one had a thin, high-arched nose. If I closed my eyes, I saw them as identical; eyes open, I could see the differences. Jason had a bad bruise in the center of his forehead, with abrasion and bleeding.

I turned to the notes on his family but again the *Sourdough* had covered the story pretty well. I jotted down, as before, ages of the parents and the father's military history. I wondered if Dennis Wheeler could arrange for me to have copies of the pictures of the two boys with their eyes open. I could come to doubt the evidence of my eyes unless I had the proof of their startling resemblance before me.

I opened the third file. How do other writers live with death? How do they live with tragedy day and night? I suppose the fact that most mystery writers create imaginary people, and that the ones they kill off are usually unsavory characters whom everyone wants dead anyway, makes some difference. I wasn't sure I was up to poring over pictures of another dead male child.

I forced myself to do it, and there looking up at me was a third golden-haired, blue-eyed boy. So very like the other two, yet so very different. If I hadn't been seated, I think I would have fallen to the floor. I was weak, dizzy, and, I think, in shock. I don't know how long I sat there. It may have been only ten minutes, but it felt like hours before I was able to go through the file in anything like an organized fashion.

William de Forest Hodgson had disappeared on April 7, and his partially frozen body was found on the Chena River bank near Alaskaland on May 10. It must have been trapped somewhere and released during breakup, while ice was floating down the river. I turned back to the beginning of the file.

In the first picture he appeared to be partially encased in ice. Then, after he was taken to the morgue I could see that he was wearing a red down jacket, no hat, light ski-type gloves, and tennis shoes. Under these he wore a white striped sport shirt and gray cord trousers. He had the same thin nose as the other two, and high cheekbones.

Nauseous and with trembling hands, I jotted down a few notes, gathered my belongings, and returned the files. I somehow got myself home. I should have called a taxi, but I didn't have the wit to do it. I just staggered the five blocks. I even denied myself the comfort of a cup of coffee or a hot tub; I just threw my clothes on the floor and crawled into bed. And I stayed there, all day and all night.

I dreamed about those boys. The three seemed to merge into one; that is, I didn't see them as Mark and Jason and William. They became identical triplets, each a composite of the three. They all wore blue down parkas and red knitted hats and puffy mittens and tennis shoes. I saw them in a snowball fight outside Moore Hall, a campus dormitory. I saw them skiing on the university trails. I saw them wrestling and tussling with each other, and laughing and joking and slapping each other on the back. My last vision of them, before I woke up, was of the three, standing side by side, their arms around each other's shoulders, their blue eyes all staring into mine.

Chapter 9

The chief danger, in these periods of poop is the medieval sin of Accidie: sloth, fatigue, languor, lethargy... but I said to myself, those fatal mornings, I better take out Accidie insurance.

The deaths of the three boys became something of an obsession with me. I don't mean that writing my book became an obsession. Far from it. I mean, all I really wanted to do was lie around and think about the boys: the tragedy, the grief of their parents, and eventually the strange similarities in their appearance and their backgrounds. I wanted to find out a lot more about them. I couldn't seem to get it through my thick head that I already had all the information I needed to create a piece of fiction and that I should get on with it.

Instead, for the next few days I thought about them all the time. Waking or sleeping I saw them, sometimes walking and talking together, sometimes lying separately in a deserted car by the side of the road, under the snow in the woods, or on the riverbank, encased in ice. The three of them seemed almost interchangeable, like identical triplets. You might ask how could I get so emotionally involved with three dead boys whom I never even knew, and I would have to reply, How could I not?

One morning I lay in bed, debating whether I even needed to get up. What was there to get up for? Then the phone rang. It was Abbie Buffmire, the gardening Oyster who was also a recycling Oyster, reminding me that we had an appointment with the mayor. I had made the appointment, she reminded me. It was a milestone in our lives; Marian Aldrich, the other recycling Oyster, and I had been trying for months to get the mayor interested in recycling. We three believe, at least we had believed—I wasn't sure at that moment what I believed—that in order to save the planet we had to stop wasting our resources, stop destroying goods that might still be of use to someone, anyone.

Our city dump is a disgrace. All kinds of usable things are destroyed there daily. When I make my dump runs with the winter's pickings from my empty lot, and all of my garbage that can't be recycled, invariably I have a full load on the return trip. Truthfully, we're not supposed to take anything away from the dump, so we usually go in pairs; one person engages the attention of the dump's Lord High Executioner while the other person loads the plunder. We launder and repair usable items of clothing, if necessary, and distribute them to the thrift stores.

When the Trans-Alaska Pipeline was finished the situation was really shocking. Many of the temporary residents who came here to get rich working on the pipeline took their wads of money and left. But first they hauled furniture, appliances, expensive winter gear, and household items to the dump. Those were busy days for Abbie and Marian and me, rescuing and redistributing.

So I couldn't very well tell Abbie I was too busy, since the whole project was my idea. But I no longer seemed to give a damn. I just wanted to be left alone with my misery. Nevertheless, I agreed to meet her and Marian at the mayor's office, as planned, wearing all recycled clothing, also as planned. We hoped to demonstrate to the mayor rather forcefully the quality of the goods being destroyed every day at the dump. Unfortunately, Abbie decided to wear everything all at once, and some items must have been rather recent acquisitions; they needed dry cleaning and pressing. She wore jacket over sweater over blouse, belted, with gobs of costume jewelry and even a wide-brimmed felt hat that looked as if the baler might have had a go at it before she did.

Marian looked a little better. Her ancient silk dress hung down only a few inches below her rusty cashmere coat, and if she hadn't plastered on so much makeup, she could have passed for someone's dotty maiden aunt. I wore a simple beige tweed suit, white blouse, and walking shoes, which, I flattered myself, had the well-worn look preferred by women detectives in British mysteries.

If I could have disassociated myself from the other two I would have. I don't know what ailed the mayor. He looked as if he were enjoying some huge joke, which he was never courteous enough to share with us. Anyway, we delivered our spiel and I got them out of there as fast as I could. The other two were certain our visit was a great success and that the mayor was at that very minute calling a meeting of his staff to announce a new recycling program. I thought it more likely that he was making some coarse joke at our expense. I declined their invitation to lunch and went home.

I spent the day after the jolly visit to the mayor alternately poring over my notes and lying around brooding. I wished I could contact the families of the three boys to get more background information, but I quickly dismissed that idea. I wouldn't think of forcing them to relive all that tragedy just because I was on an ego trip.

Then I realized something I should have picked up before: the three boys were not only born in Alaska, they were born on Eielson Air Force Base, and the three families had been in residence at approximately the same time. I didn't have the exact dates of their tours of duty, nor could I think of a way to get that information, so I couldn't be absolutely certain. But I had been wishing for evidence of some sort of tie among the boys, and there it was. There was even a possibility that the families might have known each other. Three tall blond mothers may have pushed baby carriages containing robust blond baby boys; perhaps they took walks together They could even have sat in the same waiting room at monthly baby clinics, shared babysitters, or discussed their hopes and dreams for their offspring.

What else might they have shared? That thought was uncalled for. I was ashamed of myself.

I moped around the house all evening, soaked for a while and went to bed, but not to sleep. My poor brain tried all night to make sense of the fact that three blond boys, born to officers' families on a subarctic air force outpost during an eighteen-month period, died violent deaths eighteen years later, over a similar period of time, not far from that same military outpost. There had to be some logical reason for the striking resemblance among the boys. Whatever it was, it could be the element that tied the boys together, the reason the imaginary murderer had to kill the three of them. My mind refused to settle on what that might be.

I was no ball of fire the next morning. Still in my robe, unkempt and uncombed when my son Rowe dropped in for lunch, as he occasionally does, I could see he was shocked. At first glance he probably thought I was sick, but a few probing questions revealed the truth. What *was* the truth?

There was no food in the house. I didn't even have a can of soup I could warm up for him. No fresh bread, no eggs, no fruit. The sink was full of dirty dishes, the kitchen floor unswept. I apologized for the condition of the house; I was concentrating on my book.

"I understand perfectly, Mother," he said, soothingly. "Your book is very important."

I searched his face for signs that he was mocking me, but found none.

"Alice and I are afraid you are overdoing it. She'll be here after work to help you with some housework, and Andrew and I will cut the grass and do some yard work."

What could I do? I groaned inwardly and forced a smile as I accepted his generous offer. God save me from dutiful sons. Thus encouraged, he went on.

"We'll clean up your shed, too. Someone made a mess of it."

With that pronouncement he left, probably to grab a hamburger somewhere on the way back to work.

Well, I certainly didn't want my daughter-in-law poking around in my house. I made an appointment with my hairdresser for late afternoon, then I washed the dirty dishes and the kitchen floor. I made my bed, hung up some clothes, and dusted and vacuumed the living room. I could see that if I was to have any peace I would have to do enough housework to keep Rowe and Alice at bay.

I greeted my rescuers looking quite rehabilitated: freshly coifed, wearing a cashmere sweater (recycled), and slacks, ditto, that still had a decent crease. I'm sure I destroyed Rowe's credibility with Alice. Served him right for meddling.

We dined on the fried chicken they brought, and as Alice and I dawdled over coffee, she told me that she and Rowe were expecting a baby. They had long been wanting another child. Andrew, though, was completely opposed to the idea of a sibling, especially a girl sibling.

"If that baby's a girl, there's going to be war," he'd threatened, when they told him the news. If he thought his parents would retract the announcement and cancel the order, he was sadly mistaken. But they were worried. I hoped Alice would get her girl, a sweet, pretty girl like Alice herself, not another boy with a bristly carrot top and a bristly disposition.

I said I would do everything in my power to help us all get through the following months. Andrew is a very stubborn character; I didn't expect him to change his stance very soon.

Rowe and Andrew ran the lawn tractor and completed the job I had started in the shed. When they were finished I had only to take the pickup load to the recycling center. So much for officious relations. I know Rowe meant well, but I hoped his hyperactive sense of responsibility wasn't going to become a nuisance. I much preferred Andrew's offhand treatment.

I took a well-earned hot soak and went to bed early. That took care of my new hairdo, but I slept like a top, whatever that means, and my dreams didn't have a single blond visitor all night.

I breakfasted on the eggs, bacon, and grapefruit I found in the fridge and had milk in my coffee for a change. Then, as I sat down to do a little dispassionate thinking about my book, the telephone rang. My mother was angry, depressed, and afraid. She had left the house for a short walk, and when she returned, she found several suitcases and a pile of her belongings on the patio, and she was locked out. She'd gone to the nearest neighbors, who called the police; a delegation showed up immediately. They persuaded my father to let Mother into the house. The police then told both of them that they did not want to receive any more such calls from the Carlisle family. There was definitely an implied threat, she said, and I better come out there right away and straighten out the old fool.

I didn't think I could straighten out either one of them. I could either break my word and put them in a retirement home, or I could do one more temporary patch-up job and leave them as they were. But I had to go out there, now.

I sat down with pad and paper to make a pretravel list. At least my recent flurry of housework was a step in the right direction.

❋ ❋ ❋ ❋ ❋ ❋

Five days later, a pair of college students cum lovers cum house-sitters were occupying my spare bedroom and Popsie was occupying a berth at our friendly boarding kennel. With my pockets bulging with Lovejoy and Kate Fansler mysteries, my carry-on bag full of notes and paper for my book, and my mind harboring the hope that maybe, just maybe, I might get a little writing done during the next three weeks, I took a taxi to the airport and began the long haul to Vermont.

Chapter 10

Had I dreamed or invented a phantom?
I think perhaps he's more real than I am.

I left for Anchorage on an early morning flight, about a fifty-minute trip. There I would change for Seattle, where I would change for LaGuardia, where I would change for Burlington, Vermont, where I would take a bus for the last thirty miles to St. Albans.

I took out Lovejoy and settled down to read. The opening lines, as usual, were typical Lovejoy.

> Betty dived with a muted shriek behind the trestle table. I couldn't blame her. I too thought it was her husband for a second. Trust Tinker to interrupt the one chance Betty and I had, even if it was in the middle of our village's annual fair.

Even before starting to write my mystery I was a student of first lines. My favorite in all literature is: "It is a truth universally acknowledged, that a single man in possession of a good fortune must be in want of a wife." Of course Jane Austen got the idea from someone named Hymenaeus, who wrote "I was known to possess a fortune and to want a wife."

I started to read Lovejoy, but for once he failed me; the adventures of Heather Adams, detective, seemed more compelling. Once aboard my second flight, I had three hours to kill until Seattle. The stewardess gave me a short reprieve by delivering a plate of French toast and bacon. During breakfast I thought about how I would pass the time if I wasn't going to read Lovejoy. After my tray was removed I lay back and closed my eyes, but not to sleep. I found myself wondering what kind of person would kill, cold-bloodedly murder, three beautiful boys. If I really tried, could I possibly project myself into the mind of a killer? I'd give it a try.

To get myself into a creative mode I lowered my seat back and did a couple of relaxation exercises: I softly told my body,

my feet are relaxed

my ankles are relaxed

my knees are relaxed

my legs are relaxed

my heart and lungs are relaxed

my head is relaxed, and so on until my entire body was completely limp. After about five minutes I was in a drowsy state. I was chanting my mantra quietly to myself when I realized that my seatmate, a woman about my age, was looking at me with alarm. I closed my eyes again and silently concentrated on descending the seventy-two steps to the University of Alaska visitor's parking lot. I relaxed so well that I fell asleep before I reached the bottom. So much for trying to be the murderer.

Waking when the plane gave a slight jolt, I told my mind to get back to business. Perhaps I could resurrect some of my favorite killers. At home in my study is a shelf of my favorite mysteries, but they are not my favorites necessarily because of the murderers. Why are they my favorites? I tried to visualize the books on the mystery shelf. The first that come to mind are *The Daughter of Time* and *Brat Ferrar* by Josephine Tey, and *Gaudy Night* by Dorothy Sayers, both writers whom I admire for their literate style of writing. Sayers, in addition to her successful Peter Wimsey detective novels, translated Dante and wrote religious plays. Josephine Tey (Elizabeth MacKintosh) was a successful playwright as well as the author of some of the "best mysteries of all time," according to the *New York Times*. I guess what drew me to these authors was their intelligence. Everything about the books was interesting and challenging, but I don't remember the murderers. Not those murderers. But there are murderers who do come to mind, like Iago, who made a murderer out of Othello and caused the death of an innocent woman. And Macbeth, who rushed to murder with his own hands, for personal gain, for power.

Then there are the Napoleon Bonaparte mysteries by Arthur Upfield, although in his case, it wasn't Upfield's erudition but his brilliant half-aborigine detective, Bony; his use of fantastic, even freakish settings all over the Australian outback; the unbearably hot, dry climate; and his knowledge of the Australian aborigines that fascinated his readers. Harvard University is said to have used the Bony books in their anthropology classes. I remember the weird landscapes and the aborigines much more clearly than I do the murderers.

I think I have more in common with Arthur Upfield than I do with those learned ladies. Like Australia, Alaska is isolated: a vast, wild place, largely unsettled, with an extremely cold climate and long dark winters.

I can't seem to get myself into the mind of a murderer, nor can I produce a satisfactory murderer as a model. Perhaps I can create a murderer to fit my specs. What kind of person do I need?

First of all, I need someone who has lived in Alaska for a long time, who lives near the university, who perhaps works there, and who knows every inch of the campus and of Fairbanks. This person is physically active, a quiet, reclusive sort who appears to be happy. Happy enough, anyway. He has great confidence in his intellect. Perhaps other people do not realize how intelligent he is. Perhaps he has done things in the past that have proved to him that he is smarter than other people. Or if he is known as an intellectual, probably no one would ever associate him with violence, let alone murder. No one would connect him with these boys, either.

He is used to living in the quiet of his mind, however he may appear to other people. So when he decides, for whatever reason, to commit a murder, no one around him sees any change in his work habits, his behavior, his moods. So what happened to this quiet, unobtrusive citizen to turn him into a murdering fiend?

One day, on the University of Alaska campus, he sees a tall, golden-haired freshman who instantly changes his life: he is Mark, the boy who ostensibly committed suicide. Does he know this boy from someplace? Does the boy know him? Does the boy know something that could injure this person or someone dear to him?

In Alaska we have a few residents who come here when they are released from prison, thinking this would be a good place to start over. I'm sure some of them succeed, but we never hear about them. We only hear about the ones who revert to the behavior that sent them to prison, the ones who murder a friendly neighbor or rob a bank or convenience store. Does my murderer have a past he wants kept secret at all costs? A past that this young student may be privy to?

He sees the boy every day, or almost every day, often enough that the boy becomes a very disturbing element in—I need to give him a name—X's life. He becomes more than a constant irritation; he becomes an obsession. He follows the boy around, he anticipates his actions, he memorizes his schedule, he studies him. He wants that boy out of here. But of course he can't just say to him, "I hate you. Get out of here!" He has to make him leave. He wants the bastard dead. He will have to kill him.

But why? Why must he kill him? Why would anyone want to kill a beautiful, bright, blond boy? Damn the alliteration. Let's try means. I'll just put it in the first person, it's easier.

I have decided to kill that boy. He and I cannot coexist on the same campus or even in the same town. He infuriates me. Every time I see him, my blood pressure rises; I start to perspire, to tremble. So how did he end up dead, in his little car on Yankovich Road?

Consensus was that he drove there and parked in order to commit suicide. Actually, I, X, the murderer, lured him there. How did I do it? What did he need that I could dangle before him? What do all college kids need? Money. Yes. I run an ad in the *Daily Sourdough*, or the student newspaper—I must check on that—specifying "college student, male" for some odd jobs around my house. Or maybe I play it safe and don't specify the sex. Mark answers the ad.

"My house is hard to find," I tell him, over the phone. "I'll meet you at the country club, and you can follow me in your car." I am careful not to say anything that might lead to me, in case he repeats it to anyone else. Mark follows my instructions.

I park my car behind the building. When he arrives I'm waiting for him, but he doesn't see me. I'm lurking somewhere in the shadows—in the dark, actually—it's early December. I walk over to his little car, he opens the door, and before he can get out, I deal him a blow that knocks him unconscious. Perhaps more than one blow.

Setting the scene for suicide—this alliteration is getting out of control—I slide a hose through the right front window, I plug the leaks with insulation, and I slip the other end of the hose over the exhaust pipe. I hang around for a while, inconspicuously, until I'm sure the boy won't regain consciousness before the carbon monoxide has done its work. Then I go back to my car. When there are no other cars in sight, with headlights off I depart, mission accomplished. My world is back to normal. I am safe, or someone dear to me is safe. Until one year later, when Jason appears.

Early in the fall, just after registration, I see another tall blond boy walking across the campus, or eating in Wood Center, or in my office, or at a play/concert/game, just like Mark. I, Heather, remember my reaction when I opened the second police file to the middle and thought I was looking at another picture of Mark, only it was Jason. So I, X, am shocked.

"What are you doing here? I killed you. You have been dead and buried for almost a year." After I calm down—I'm such a stoic, such a private person, that no one notices any difference in my behavior, not a year ago, not now—I watch Jason. I stalk him. I find ways to be in places where he is sure to be. Eventually I convince myself of what I knew all along: this boy is not Mark, risen from his grave, but another boy who closely resembles Mark, and who is as much a threat to me, or my loved one, as Mark ever was. I must commit another murder.

I speculate that like Mark, Jason could use some extra money. By mid-November I am ready. I place an ad, as I did before, and Jason responds. I tell him, too, that my house is near the end of the ski trail, on Yankovich Road, and if he'll ski there, I'll be waiting.

I know something about Jason by now; I know that he is a very good skier and will certainly be coming around the ski trail at a good clip. I, Heather, skied once on that trail. Never again. The students came around the curves so fast they scared me to death. Jason does the same thing; he hurtles down the trail in proper style, and there I am, X, waiting in the middle of his path, at a carefully selected spot: a blind curve with several large birch trees on either side. He cannot ski around me, he will not ski into me; so gallant Jason leaves the trail and crashes into one of the large birches.

He hits his head hard, and falls down, stunned. I, X, wearing a ski mask, ski over to him, and deal a second blow to his head, right on the spot already abraded and bleeding from the impact with the tree. I use the weapon I have brought for that purpose, perhaps the same one I used on Mark. I ski over to Jason, carefully staying in his tracks, and scatter snow all over him, just enough to camouflage his presence in the gathering dusk. Perhaps I wait in the shadows until I am sure he will not awaken, prepared to deal another blow if necessary. And of course, Providence is on my side; no other skiers interrupt our rendezvous. I am prepared to pass myself off as a rescuer, in the event another skier shows up. Elated that my careful planning has succeeded once more, I leave Jason to freeze to death. Again Providence lends a hand: there is a light snowfall during the night.

My peace of mind is restored once more. I am relieved, safe, even complacent. I never think of my two victims. Or do I occasionally take out my bludgeon, and gloat over its efficiency? Do I long for a chance to use it again? Do I ever consider using it on someone else, just to keep in practice, or for the thrill, since no blond boys have shown up lately? Or do I kill only out of necessity?

A year later, another blond boy does show up. My response to this blond presence on campus is more measured. I don't have a violent physical reaction the first time I see him; I don't have to follow him everywhere; I don't have to settle in my mind that he is a threat. I recognize him at first sight as one of a seemingly endless band of blond brothers—damn—who insist on threatening, even torturing me and/or someone I love, and I am prepared not only to murder him, but this time I will do it in a more audacious way than ever before. I have pulled off one successful suicide and one successful accident. What will the next one be?

When I have had sufficient time to plan a new and daring *modus operandi*, I place the usual ad, in the usual place, and he responds, in the usual way. Also in the usual way, we agree to meet. And so, with the usual dispatch, another fine young man dies. My only regret is that no one will ever appreciate my cleverness, my creativity, my expertise.

I, Heather, cannot begin to speculate on how the third murder was committed. The third boy, William, disappeared, and he either died immediately or was held prisoner somewhere for almost a month. I think he was probably killed immediately or that he was knocked out and placed somewhere to freeze to death. I think these were distinctly Alaskan murders, by a killer who knew how to use the means at hand, the death-dealing arctic cold. But what icy sepulchre held his body during the ensuing month, and how was his frozen body unobtrusively transported to the river?

I think I have finally created a satisfactory murderer. No doubt he'll change and develop as I progress further into the book. Years of reading mysteries and of paying particular attention to sensational murder cases have given me a unique opportunity to formulate some theories about murderers. They may be everyone else's theories too, or they may be absolutely crazy, but here they are.

From time to time there have been murder cases that have dominated the media. Let's say a well-known professional man comes home to find that someone has brutally murdered his wife and children during his absence. Or perhaps he was at home, but somehow managed to sleep through the carnage.

The man, the bereaved father and husband, has no acceptable alibi and there may be other suspicious signs, so he is eventually charged with the murders. According to the Heather Adams theory, most innocent people, if they truly loved their families, would be devastated over their loss; they might have a mental breakdown, or they could be emotionally crippled for some time, even for life. They could lose their interest in living, in sex, in their work.

If a man who had just lost his family by such brutal means were also to be charged with their deaths, he would be an extraordinarily strong person if he were able to retain any mental or emotional equilibrium at all. When I read of an accused husband or father who, during the period of investigation or while awaiting trial for the murders or during the period between trials, if there are more than one, is involved in high living, in a lively social life, and multiple affairs with women, I think to myself, "man, you are guilty. You don't care at all that your wife and babes are in their graves, and that you put them there."

An innocent person who has lost his or her family, by whatever means, cannot get on with his life, not for a long time, if ever. When we see one of these miraculous recoveries, especially when the bereaved person is also the accused killer, it behooves us to examine the previous life of that person. Of course, this is not always possible, but to Heather Adams, detective, anything is possible. So I will tell you what we would find.

We would find that the accused killer, husband, father, had shown signs of a lack of feeling for living creatures, human or animal, going way back in his life, perhaps even to his childhood. He was probably adept at getting what he wanted; his needs always came first, over siblings, parents, wife, children. He was an accomplished liar, and nothing was too small, or too big, to lie about. If he was occasionally caught in one of his lies, he didn't care.

I decided long ago that people don't change, even in something as superficial as organization work. We've all had the experience of working with a person who doesn't keep commitments or who really botches up whatever he is supposed to do, time after time. We become wary of working with that person. It isn't always possible to come right out and say, "I won't work with him or her, he's a complete screw-up." But we learn to exert a bit of damage control the second time around, and if the pattern is the same, we see to it that there isn't a third time.

With crimes of passion, if I may continue with the Heather Adams theory, we have a one-time killer who never meant or wanted to kill, who lost control in a moment of passion, and this person is usually devastated by what he has done; as often as not he turns himself in to the police. Even if he is acquitted, he does not acquit himself and continues to live with his guilt all the days of his life, which may never mean much to him again.

This is not a good comparison, but if you have ever known someone who has lost a child, he often blames himself for the death. What could he/she have done differently that might have saved the child's life? And in those cases where a parent has accidentally caused the death of a child by averting his attention for the few seconds it takes for a toddler to drown in his bath, or electrocute himself, or run behind a backing car, that parent often has a terrible struggle to retain his sanity. A normal human being does not want to kill anyone.

Several small children died when they built a snow fort in the middle of a road. The snow was deep, and there was no way the snowplow operator could have seen them. The unfortunate man broke down completely and had to be hospitalized. I would wager that he has not enjoyed a single guilt-free day since that unhappy event, and he was clearly innocent of the deaths.

Something else about my killer of the first type: he may have a brilliant mind, he may even be outstanding in his chosen field, but some very important piece has been omitted from his psyche. He can't express normal human emotions because he doesn't feel them, so he has to simulate. If a situation arises that seems to call for a display of emotion, this person does not simply react spontaneously. No, he has to stop and think, "How should I react in this situation? How does a bereaved husband/father act?" He thinks back over instances where he has observed other bereft people, and he chooses one to emulate. Sometimes he gets it wrong; his behavior is inappropriate. That's the dead giveaway: inappropriate responses.

These people are very interesting with all their contradictions. Sometimes they have charisma and a willingness to court publicity. Many articles have been written about them, and a few books. Needless to say, this is the kind of killer I am going to create for my book, because, to my mind, hardly any reason would have been sufficient to cause a normal person to murder three fine boys. Those killings were not accidents, nor were they done in the heat of passion. They were carefully conceived and carried out by someone who considered himself to be outside all the rules of human behavior; laws like "Thou shalt not kill" simply did not apply. And my killer would have a long history of ego-centered behavior, maybe even of secret, petty crimes. Or not-so-petty crimes.

Two thousand years ago Juvenal said, *"Nemo repente fuit turpissimus."* No one ever becomes extremely wicked suddenly. My sentiments exactly.

As I read back over my notes I find that half the time I speak of the deaths of the boys as if they were actual murders and of the killer as if he were a real person, instead of a figment of my imagination. I seem also to assume that the murderer is a male. I suppose that is natural, even logical. If I am correct in any of my suppositions, only a strong man could have delivered the blows that knocked two boys unconscious long enough for one to die of carbon monoxide poisoning, and the other to freeze to death. I don't know any woman capable of striking such a blow, or of transporting the frozen body of a large young male from the site of the murder to the river. Nor do I believe any woman could kill three handsome boys who might have been her own sons. But men, like male animals, are different. I've known a number of stepfathers who were unable to accept their wife's children from a previous marriage and who abused the children fearfully. Recently there's been a rash of child murders by live-in boyfriends. In the wild, male bears will often kill any cub they find without its mother. Women don't do things like that. Not that women are always ideal stepparents, but I think numbers are in their favor.

I hear the slight change in the timbre of the engines that signals our descent into Seattle. I quickly jot down my thoughts about the killer, and as I sit there looking over my notes I begin to shake, overtaken by a violent chill. By defining the murderer, by walking in his footsteps, I have somehow created him; he has become real. I have created such a monster that I am afraid of him. If I tear up my notes, will he go away?

Chapter 11

Me, I like books that encourage the mind to wander....
Digressions... are the sunshine of literature.

In the Seattle airport I decided to get a little exercise. I put my carry-on and purse into a locker and did slow laps up and down the vast concourses. Very decorous laps. I tried for once to concentrate on my parents but their problems seemed to defy solution. They would be getting along very well, even now, if it were not for their eccentricities. I pondered the matter during twenty whole minutes of lapping, then went to a private airline club to rest my old bones on something soft.

I wanted to stay away from my newly created murderer, so I picked up my Amanda Cross novel, pseudonymously written by a Columbia University professor of English. One of her books caused me some small embarrassment, but at least it was private embarrassment. Her heroine-detective, Kate Fansler, also a professor of English, stated that many graduate students attempt to write a sequel to Jane Austen's *Pride and Prejudice*.

I was, of course, long past the age of her graduate students, but there in my desk drawer at home lay a short story, perhaps more of a vignette, depicting what might have taken place between spirited Elizabeth Bennet and the very reserved Mr. Darcy during the lengthy drive from Elizabeth's home at Longbourn to Darcy's townhouse in London following their wedding. Not exactly a sequel to *P and P*, but close enough to make me squirm. I like to read between the lines and fill in something that the author chose to leave to the reader's imagination. Finding a plot for a sequel to *Pride and Prejudice* would be a problem, because Darcy and Elizabeth were obviously destined for an exemplary, serene married life, unless a widowed Mrs. Bennet took it in her head to move in with them. Now that would be worth writing.

"Professor Kate Fansler mounted the stairs to the upper campus where the azalea bushes were just coming into bud." I don't think I'd add that to my collection of great first lines. My long acquaintance with Kate lured me on, but the next thing I knew the attendant, an attractive girl with short black hair, was bending over me, telling me it was time to go to my departure gate. I had slept a whole hour, but at least it was an hour free from thoughts of dead boys and my murderous creation.

Happily I had another direct flight, to La Guardia, three and a half hours. I looked around the cabin of this very large plane. For the three-hour plus flights to and from Alaska we don't have these huge double-decked aeronautical leviathans, with their vast twelve-seat-abreast cabins. I settled as comfortably as I could in the narrow seat—the seats and leg space aren't any roomier—and took out a book, to rob my new seatmate of any excuse to open a conversation. I noticed she had a book too. I gave up on Kate Fansler, but holding on to the book as a diversionary tactic, I went back to my own mystery.

I lay back and closed my eyes. What about my lack of a "closed society?" Perhaps I could solve that problem on this leg of the trip. Mentally I pictured meetings of every group or club I belonged to—quite a number, since Alaskans are compulsive joiners. It must be something to do with the long dark winters. I pictured again the Unitarians, the American Association of University Women, the Retired Teachers, the National Organization for Women, the Democratic Party. I doubted that any members of those organizations would relish seeing their counterparts murdering and being murdered.

The Unitarians were a possibility; I can't imagine any one of them getting angry about being picked to be a murderer—different name, of course—as long as I picked a murderer with a sense of humor.

The Unitarians would probably want to appoint a couple of committees to help me choose the murderer. Or take a vote. I really need a smaller closed society. There would be more Unitarian suspects than I could handle, and I wouldn't dare leave anyone out.

I forgot the Oysters. Well, what about the Oysters? Before rejecting the idea out of hand, consider: there are only nine Oysters, a manageable number. They are interesting, mildly eccentric characters, and they all live or work at or near the university. I should be able to contrive reasons for the various Oysters to get to know the three boys. They all like young men. So does Marian's Doctor. I wonder if Joan's doctor likes young men.

Most of the Oysters have part-time help for yard work and snow shoveling. Abbie Buffmire hires someone to help with her big garden and so do the Williams sisters, with all their cat boxes. Katie George, I think, gets a lot of help from her army of relations, but Florence Hokkainen has a special *tendre* for handsome young men and plenty of work for them to do. And who knows, the Oysters might enjoy being characters in a book, even a book doomed from its birth to blush unseen.

The more I thought about it, the more I liked the idea. The Oysters had already shown a lot of interest in my book, they knew I was going to use the actual stories of the three boys, and they certainly knew that having decided to write the book, I would finish it. Yes, I would use the Oysters as my closed society. I should be able to make a murderer out of one of them and a good bunch of suspects out of the others. The only problem was that I felt certain the murderer was a male, but I could use the Oysters as red herrings until I found him.

The stewardess slid a hot meal in front of me, a chicken casserole with salad and a small piece of cake. I was ready for it. By the time the tray was cleared away another hour had flown. I had just enough time to add the Oysters to my notes before hearing the telltale warning of our final descent. I gathered my paraphernalia and prepared to leave the plane at LaGuardia.

Chapter 12

Like the grave digger in Hamlet I call a spade a spade.

What a crowded place La Guardia airport is. I wanted to do some laps but had to settle for a slow meander. I had forty-five minutes to kill, then a forty-minute flight to Burlington, Vermont, where I would take a forty-minute bus ride to St. Albans, then a twenty-minute taxi ride and I would be there. *There* is a late eighteenth-century calico stone house on Lake Champlain, almost a twin to Washington's headquarters at Valley Forge. The grounds are complete with maple trees, a huge vegetable garden, and a lake boat, which like the hearing aid batteries, is being carefully preserved. I usually manage to sneak it out of the barn at least once every trip, when Father is otherwise engaged, but not, I think, this trip.

There is nothing quite like visiting one's parents to lop years off one's age. I feel like a teen-ager when I go home. There's something else; eighty makes sixty look young. It's almost comical. Possibly it's something like a Relative Wrinkle Quotient. And I must always remember to bring white gloves and a hat, in case we're invited out to tea, and I must never offer to chop firewood or paint the kitchen. They brought me up to be a lady, and a lady I must be, around them.

I packed up the two of them as fast as I could and got them out of the house. It wasn't as easy as it sounds. When I automatically took the driver's seat Father announced that "the girl" and I could go; he wasn't coming unless he could drive. I told him that I got a headache if I sat

69

anywhere but in the driver's seat. Marvin the geologist's stratagem worked again. Father didn't want his baby girl to have a headache.

The car offered silent evidence of the current state of Father's driving. It looked bird-shot all over, but especially in the rear. He backs out into busy traffic with great abandon. Whenever he connects with a passing motorist, he simply pulls out his wallet and asks, "How much is this going to cost me?" He has made the day for many a Vermonter with one of these brief encounters.

We spent several days around Boothbay Harbor, in Maine, where we did a bit of bathing and beachcombing. After a few days of rest, fresh lobster, and beautiful coastal panoramas, we were all more relaxed. Those two old folks are in remarkably good physical condition. Gardening and midnight strolls and dips in the lake must be excellent preservatives.

I got them to take naps, and while one napped, I talked with the other. During my session with Mother, we discussed Father's driving. She insisted that he be forbidden to drive, but since she didn't drive anymore, that opened up a whole new can of worms; without a driver they wouldn't be able to shop in St. Albans, eight miles away. They'd be forced to move out of their long-time home. I don't think she could see that far ahead. I suggested that she let Father do the shopping, but she didn't like that idea either.

I tried to persuade each one that they would have to make an effort to get along, to help each other instead of squabbling all the time. If they were to continue locking each other out and forcing the police to settle their disputes, they would leave me no other option but to put them in a retirement home. Or take them to live with me in Alaska. That last threat did it.

By the time we got back to Vermont Father seemed to accept the fact that he was not going to get his long-lost wife back, that "the girl" was all he could expect, and he'd better make the best of it. Mother agreed to accept the changes in Father. These two, who had become virtual strangers, would have to cohabit peacefully if they wanted to stay on in their own home.

In happier days, they used to joke about how I got my first name. They'd honeymooned in Scotland, and nine months later they'd christened me Heather, after the purple mound on which I'd been conceived. Which probably explains why I had no siblings. No heather.

I spent the next two weeks cleaning house and taking loads to the dump in Father's old pickup, hoping no police would notice the expired license plates. I spent several days going through their checking accounts and bills, and I arranged for a woman to come in twice weekly to clean—Father had fired the last one when he couldn't find the can opener. And I formally hired the neighboring teenager to look in on my parents twice every day. His parents kindly assured me that they too would keep an eye on them, also for a fee.

We had final trips to the beauty parlor and the barber, more trips to the podiatrist, dentist, and their doctor. I took them, singly, on shopping trips to refurbish their wardrobes, since I had thrown out most of their clothes. The night before I left, we went out to the local version of Ye Olde New England Inn where we had a fine dinner, the like of which none of us saw very often anymore.

We had a tearful parting. They had been generous, easygoing parents, and I owed them the same consideration. But none of my options felt as if they would bring joy, or even a minimum of contentment, to any of us. Perhaps there was none to be had.

I had nothing to show for the trip back. I slept all the way to Seattle. When I was sufficiently recovered I read the whole of the Lovejoy book between Seattle and Anchorage. Between Anchorage and Fairbanks I thought about the Oysters. First of all, I wasn't going to tell them they were the closed society, at least until I had made some impromptu visits and written character sketches of each one. Then I would settle down to some serious writing. The Oysters would reconvene in late September, and I wanted to have something really impressive for the first meeting. Our motto, *Insanabile cacoethes scribendi*, an incurable itch to write, may have been a joke to Juvenal, but it is no laughing matter to the Oysters. Actually, Juvenal was rather unkind. "An inveterate and incurable itch for writing besets many and grows old in their sick hearts" would be a more accurate translation. When I suggested the motto, I gave the Oysters my shortened version.

Chapter 13

Summer plunges on ... we have killed July.

Perhaps August is the cruelest month, after all. April has some redeeming features, but August has none. All over the United States people are enjoying sunshine and ninety-degree temperatures and lolling around on beaches, while we poor stupid Alaskans are sloshing around in rain and mud. Nine summers out of ten we have rain the whole month of August. If I have to make a trip down to America, I try to do it in August, because it is the one month of the year when I wonder what I'm doing here.

I must admit that when I sound off on this subject, someone always contradicts me, and says that August is not a miserable, rainy month, although lately I've heard people referring to August as the monsoon season. August seems to be a matter of opinion. One of these days I'll check the almanac and settle the matter. But I just spent all of July in sunny Vermont, and I would now spend all of August here getting very wet from that controversial rain.

I no sooner got home than the August deluge began. I paid off the young lovers who, as usual, had taken good care of my house. I had a joyous reunion with Popsie the poodle, and then later with Alice and Rowe and Andrew. It would have been more joyous if Andrew hadn't looked so glum. The signs of his mother's advancing pregnancy were reminding him that his days as an only child were numbered; that the threat of an infant sibling, particularly a female infant sibling, would not go away by ignoring it.

Alice looked tired. I invited Andrew for a visit, and he accepted. Damn. I'd done it again. I'll have to entertain Andrew and his fiends (that is a typo, but leave it), prepare regular meals, and god knows what else.

I immediately reactivated the old Family Book Club. I offered Andrew fifty cents for each book he read, subject to my approval. He looked at me pityingly.

"It's like taking candy from a baby, Gram," he said, smiling craftily. "I'm a fast reader. You're going to go broke."

I smiled back just as craftily. "It will be worth the money."

I threw out most of the mail and newspapers unopened. Well, I did pick out a notice from the library that the Alvarez and Camus books on suicide were overdue. I hated to part with them, so I solved the problem by ordering used copies from Powell's in Portland.

Later Andrew and I sat down to talk about our separate and combined agendas. We agreed that I would spend my mornings writing and Andrew would spend his reading. If I had to pay an afternoon call—I planned to start visiting the Oysters—he would visit selected friends. All of Andrew's friends seem to have been carefully selected. That was the problem.

If the damned rain would ever let up we could do some yard work or go down to the lake. Meanwhile, when not reading or visiting, we would play chess, or checkers, or poker. Or just see what Fortune decreed. When Andrew is around, Fortune sometimes seems a bit hyperactive.

For our first morning I prepared the gargantuan breakfast that Andrew never gets at home but seems to expect here. I made what Andrew calls my Killer Pancake. It is baked in the oven in an iron skillet, and puffs up to great size.

The recipe:

Killer Pancake

1. Heat oven to 450 degrees
2. Beat together until smooth:
    ½ cup flour
    2 cups milk
    3 eggs
    ¼ tsp salt
    1 tbsp sugar
3. Melt 1 tbsp butter in iron skillet. When the butter's bubbling, pour into batter and stir. Pour batter into iron skillet.
4. Bake 10–15 min., until pancake puffs way up high.
5. Reduce temperature to 400 degrees, bake 15–20 minutes until brown.

Call boy(s) for the Presentation of the Pancake, just before it comes out of the oven. It falls very quickly. Don't make Killer Pancakes for anyone who won't get up for the Presentation. Serve with honey, maple syrup, jam, cinnamon sugar, strawberries, or be creative. WARNING: Number of young guests likely to multiply exponentially.

Andrew was on hand for the Presentation of the Pancake, as required, and in his hand was his first book club selection, *Moll Flanders.* I was not going to approve it, but I wouldn't tell him that.

"*Moll Flanders*! I haven't read that since I was a girl! What an interesting woman she grew up to be!"

"Girl? Woman? What is she, some kind of *Anne of Green Gables*?"

"I remember when your father and I had this very same discussion, Andrew. Actually, it's very educational."

"Educational? Wasn't she a gangster's moll?"

"No, Andrew, she was a poor simple girl who was abandoned by her mother when she was a baby. After many years of poverty and petty crime the girl repented. She became very religious and quite rich in her old age."

I handed the book to him, but he refused it, a look of disgust on his face. His father had decided against it, too, twenty-five years ago.

Andrew finally settled on *White Fang* by Jack London, and I went to my study to work.

From the *Sourdough* and my travel notes, I had:

Setting: Fairbanks, Alaska
Milieu: the Oysters
Victims: three college freshmen
Murderer: as described in airplane notes
Means: as described in *Sourdough*, with invented details
                  from notes
Motive: none yet
Detective :   Heather Adams (more or less)

I hadn't organized my notes on the boys; by combining my gleanings from the *Sourdough* and the police files I got:

Name: Mark Wesley Sandberg
Date of Birth: August 15, 1972
Place of birth: Eielson Air Force Base, Alaska
Father: Col. Eric Sandberg
Mother: Karen Kjellmark Sandberg
Sibling: Sonja, 16
Died: Dec. 5, 1990

Mark's father had retired from the Air Force when Mark was eighteen years old, indicating that he was not exactly young when Mark was born. Nor was his mother. He was two years old, and Sonja was just born, when Col. Sandberg was transferred to Hawaii. Subsequently Col. Sandberg served on bases in California, Florida, Germany, and England.

In high school Mark was a straight-*A* student in all his subjects, but his main interest had been science. He was also a fine athlete, excelling in soccer, hockey, and skiing.

Mark had never forgotten that he was an Alaskan. Even as a small boy he spoke of returning to his birthplace some day. At his high-school graduation in Santa Barbara he had received a number of scholastic awards and an offer of a four-year scholarship to an Ivy League college, but he'd persuaded his parents that the time had come for him to return to Alaska. He'd saved quite a bit of money for college, and the University of Alaska had an acceptable academic reputation, so his parents gave their consent.

Mark had held part-time jobs for years: in military commissaries as a bag boy, in automobile repair shops changing and repairing tires, and washing cars.

After his arrival in Alaska, Mark had maintained close contact with his parents and sister, keeping them informed about his classes; his dorm life; campus functions such as games, movies, dances, and plays; as well as the pranks he and his friends played on each other. He wrote frequent, playful letters to Sonja. In one of his last letters to his parents, just before his death, he mentioned his intention to seek part-time work. His name had been found on the lists of several campus agencies.

A boy in an adjoining room in the dormitory said that Mark had an appointment to see someone about work on the day he died, but the prospective employer never came forward. The police concluded that Mark had just invented that excuse in order to get away by himself. I didn't believe it.

Andrew came in looking famished. Where had all the pancake gone? Ah, well. I put away my notes and repaired to the kitchen. Happily, Andrew didn't have his heart set on an afternoon of wild adventure. He was willing to do yard work, if I would pay him. I could see that Andrew expected to make his fortune during this visit. The rain having let up to a drizzle, we tucked away chicken and melted cheese sandwiches and soup, donned rain gear, and went outside.

With everything so wet, we couldn't cut the grass. Instead we picked up empty liquor bottles on my vacant lot, which is a favorite shortcut for a segment of the population who cannot make the short walk to the center of town without liquid refreshment. They drop their empties on my lot, preferably on a rock, if they can find one. Deterrents like fences, mounds of dirt, and piles of branches have no effect at all. However, I get periodic exercise and the recycling center gets a few bags of bottles and cans; we took a load that afternoon. Andrew was $2.25 richer. He appeared well satisfied.

Back to the house for hot showers; that is, hot for Andrew, warm for me. It was just like having my son Rowe back. When he left home,

I lost a son but gained some hot water. I set my alarm for six and went to bed early. I trusted Andrew to do the same.

Six-fifteen the next morning found me and a cup of coffee at my typewriter. With Jason Calloway's files before me I wrote:

Name:	Jason Randolph Calloway
Date of Birth:	January 17, 1973
Place of birth:	Eielson Air Force Base, Alaska
Father:	Lt. Col. John Danforth Calloway
Mother:	Suzanne Randolph Calloway
Died:	November 26, 1991

Jason was an only child. When he was eighteen months old his father was transferred out of Alaska, and, like Mark, he spent his childhood on various military installations around the world. He had always been an excellent student and an outstanding athlete; he lettered in swimming and basketball, and he was also a good skier. He had received several local and national awards for science projects and was equally good in mathematics. Despite his acceptance at several other colleges, Jason had been adamant about returning to the state of his birth.

When he arrived on campus in early September of 1991, he was assigned a room in Bartlett Hall, which he shared with Donald Hendrickson, a freshman from Idaho. The two boys immediately built a sleeping loft, as was the custom. Jason adjusted quickly to campus life, and his classes went well. Both boys were serious scholars; nevertheless they found time to play some soccer and basketball. Jason made friends easily and was dating another freshman, Marilyn Norris, from Montana. The two hadn't known each other long, but there was no doubt that she took his death very badly.

Jason was looking for part-time work at the time of his death. Like Mark, he too had worked as a bag boy in the commissaries and had later worked for several car rental agencies. He was willing to try his hand at anything, from babysitting to house cleaning. He'd had several leads, and he'd told his roommate that he expected to see someone about work the day he died.

He must have died before he could keep the appointment, or, more likely, no specific time had been set, because no one ever came forward to say that Jason had failed to keep an appointment. But then, why would they? There had never been any question about how Jason died; it was clearly an accident, and very likely the police hadn't even delved into the matter.

Jason's parents lived in Seattle, where his father, retired from the military, was an executive with Boeing.

So far no Andrew. Good. I'll just go on to the third boy.

Name:	William de Forest Hodgson
Date of Birth:	March 23, 1973
Place of Birth:	Eielson Air Force Base
Father:	Brig. General Wayne Edward Hodgson
Mother:	Marguerite de Forest Hodgson
Sibling:	Barbara
Disappeared:	April 7, 1992
Body Found:	May 10, 1992

Brigadier Gen. Hodgson, who had been the base commander at Eielson Air Force Base, was transferred to Washington, D.C., when William was three years old. The Hodgsons adopted Barbara, a part Eskimo child, just before they left Alaska. William had attended schools in Washington, D.C., until he was twelve years old, when his father was transferred to England. There he had been enrolled in what is called a public school in Britain, but is actually a private school. About the time he was completing his secondary schooling, Brig. Gen. Hodgson decided to retire from the military. Bill had delayed his entrance into college in order to help his parents make their move from England to Texas.

Bill, like the other two boys, had been an outstanding student. He'd been offered full scholarships to Brown and Tufts, but he accepted neither; his heart was set on returning to Alaska. He'd entered the University of Alaska in January 1992, after seeing his parents settled, and had quickly adjusted to campus life. He'd had a single room in Monroe Hall and had taken his meals in the Commons. He'd enrolled in a heavier load of classes than was usual for freshmen and was also playing basketball several times a week with the varsity team, which probably would have accepted him had he been there in September. He'd gone skiing at Skiland with other students on several weekends and was talking about looking for some part-time work.

I couldn't believe the similarities among the three boys. Bill, like the other two, was outstanding in science. They were all athletic, not all that unusual in itself, I suppose; but the fact that they were all born within a fairly small area, Eielson Air Force Base, in this vast state, and had this uncanny resemblance to one another was almost too much for me to assimilate. I was reminded of a quote from Aristotle, about the Honest Mare of Pharsalus, who always bred true. The offspring of the Honest Mare always resembled the stud.

Here he is. The *Pax Andrevicus* is over. Maybe if he's in a very good mood, he'll let me look in on an Oyster or two this afternoon.

Chapter 14

I am seriously a private detective: perhaps the most private ever because I do my detecting in secret and without fee. Even my best friends have no idea of this. That is why they are my best friends.

Andrew announced, between enormous bites of Belgian waffle, that the weather was supposed to clear up on the following day, so why didn't we plan a trip to the lake? I agreed on the condition that I have this afternoon off to pay a few social calls. He said he had some social calls to make, too. CJ was to have the honor of Andrew's company for the afternoon. I telephoned CJ's mother to be sure that she had been informed of the impending honor. There was no way that I wanted those two creative geniuses alone in that house or any house for a whole afternoon. The answer was satisfactory, so we made plans to go our separate ways after lunch.

Andrew spent the morning with *White Fang* and I worked at my desk. After lunch, my first call would be on Joan Van Blarcom. If time permitted, I would also call on the Williams sisters. Without phoning ahead. I wanted my potential suspects to be as natural as possible in their home settings. If they were busy, or had guests, I would return another time.

I spent some time thinking about the victims. Why should they have been selected as the victims? In most detective fiction the victim is of bad, or at least questionable, character; the first victim, that is. Someone hates him or her enough to commit murder. The process of covering up the first murder often causes innocent people to die, because, as I pointed out before, a murderer is so ego-centered that nothing must be allowed to disturb his or her world, even if innocent people have to die to right that world. So what about the three victims? Why were they the victims?

To begin with, they were all exemplary characters, as fine sons as anyone could hope to have. They were brilliant, all three; athletic, with likeable, friendly personalities. All had had the good fortune to be born into families who obviously liked children, who wanted to be parents. Judging from the ages of the parents when their sons were born (each was a first child), they'd waited a long time to become parents.

These were not authoritarian parents; many parents would have insisted that their sons attend the Ivy League schools that had offered scholarships for them. If they had insisted, would the boys still be alive? Or would my shadowy murderer have tracked them down, wherever they were? Had other blond boys died at the hand of this killer, somewhere else? There I go again, acting as if these are real instead of hypothetical murders. Not even hypothetical: imaginary. Fictional. I'd been slipping in and out of reality ever since I started this book. Well, I would continue to do so; it seemed to be the only way I could get anything done. So what else?

The three boys were born in Alaska, on Eielson Air Force Base; they returned to Alaska from distant points in the United States and England, and of all the freshmen at the university, those three, with all their similarities, had to die. There had to have been other returning Alaska-born students who didn't die. Perhaps the place of their birth is not important. But with so much coincidence, I can't ignore it.

What else? Well, the victims seem almost to have been racially selected: perfect examples of very blond, Nordic, Aryan types. These boys were easy to spot when they set foot on campus. Anyone would have noticed them.

Someone, though, didn't like their type. Was there some neo-Nazi group operating on campus? If so, there would have been more deaths of blond students, and someone surely would have noticed. Wait. I've got it wrong: neo-Nazis would have approved of their blondness; their opposite counterpart would murder blonds. Is there such a group?

What else? All three boys were budding scientists. Important? I just don't know. And this matter of the uncanny resemblance among the three boys—I think that when the university reconvenes next month I'll spend a little time hanging around the campus to see if there are many blond students and if any of them look like Mark and Jason and Bill.

Wild horses thundering down the stairs. Time to restoke the fiery furnace that is Andrew and dress for my afternoon calls. Why do I feel that at last I am getting somewhere?

Both of us outfitted for the rain, I dropped Andrew at CJ's, escorting him to the door to verify that CJ's mother was at home. Ten minutes later I was parking in front of Joan Van Blarcom's apartment house. She answered the buzzer immediately. I wasn't especially comfortable as I made my way up the stairs to her door. I had never dropped in on her before. Here, that is, in her apartment. I used to visit their home regularly before she and Philip separated. One doesn't drop in on apartment dwellers the way one does on house dwellers. I must admit that there are only a few people on whom I pay unannounced calls. Joan is no longer one of them. We simply are not the good friends we once were.

How unlike her to be living in an apartment at all. When I first met her she was living in the big house on Yankovich Road, surrounded by cats, dogs, birds, and goodness knows what else. Then suddenly they all disappeared, and Joan said, when asked, that pets tied them down too much. I never knew to whom they gave the pets—I never asked—and I never noticed any great increase in the amount of traveling the Van Blarcoms did. I had the impression that it was, if anything, less. Something had gone terribly wrong in her life, and at one time I think she would have come to me, or Marcia, if she needed someone to talk to, but now she was keeping it all locked up inside, whatever it was. It's not easy watching an old friend living through a cataclysmic life experience, and not being able to help her. I don't believe she and Marcia were as close as they once were, either. Marcia had introduced Joan to the Oysters, years ago.

Joan quickly answered the door, looking paler, wispier, and thinner than the last time I'd seen her, which wasn't so very long ago. She was plainly surprised to see me.

She graciously took my raincoat and went to put the kettle on for tea. I couldn't help remembering the first time I had ever heard of her, on Maury Smith's radio program. Some bush pilot was lost, and private pilots were being recruited to help with the search. Joan was one of the first to volunteer. There had been a picture of Joan, Joan Underwood as she was then, on the front page of the *Sourdough*. Tall and lithe, she was standing beside her Cessna 180, with the light reflecting off her golden hair. She'd looked so brimming over with life.

Soon afterward she had married Dr. Philip Van Blarcom, a brilliant young biologist at the University of Alaska who had achieved a measure of fame for a recently published paper on insect genetics. He had also assisted in the spectacular rescue of some injured climbers on Denali. What a pair they had been when they were young; how well-matched they'd seemed, both tall and fair, both so eager for adventure.

Joan returned with a tray bearing a teapot, cups, and assorted cookies. She was much too well bred to ask me what I wanted.

"So how's the book going?" she asked as she poured.

"Just so-so. It's slowly falling into place. I have the victims, those three freshmen I've told you about; I just can't seem to think of a motive, any reason for someone to kill those three boys. But I'll think of something."

As she handed me a cup of tea her hand shook, and the cup tipped over in the saucer, slopping scalding water on my knee. Fortunately, I was wearing wool slacks, but I still received a painful, though not very large, burn.

"Oh, Heather, I'm so sorry! Take off your slacks and let me put something on that knee for you. I've got an aloe plant. Let me look ..."

"Don't bother, Joan. Forget it. It's no big deal. In fact, it's nothing at all." It hurt like hell. "I just happened to be in the neighborhood and thought I'd see how you are. I haven't talked to you since..."

"You fell in the river," she finished for me.

"Right." Thank you for reminding me.

"I've often wondered how you were doing with your... mystery. I've thought about calling you, but then, I knew I'd be finding out... soon enough." Carefully, Joan handed me a fresh cup of tea.

"That's right, we have the fall meeting of the Oysters coming up in a few weeks, and I've promised myself to have the first three chapters written. But I just can't come up with a reason for anyone to kill those three wonderful boys."

"Perhaps you should select some other victims?"

"I can't do that. I'd have to start over from scratch. I'm much too involved with these three victims. I'm going to finish this book or die in the attempt."

The instant those words were out of my mouth I knew I shouldn't have said them. In murder mysteries the next victim always says something like that, or the famous last words, "I can take care of myself." I reminded myself that this, too, was fiction. A fictional murderer couldn't kill me.

Joan, obviously upset, was staring at me.

"Heather, have you thought about what you're doing? Suppose that your book does get published. Think of the grief you'll cause the parents of those boys, having their deaths dragged up again, made the subject of a... detective story." It sounded like a dirty word, on her lips. "How can you do this to them?"

I couldn't believe my ears.

"Well, to begin with, I will be as surprised as anyone if this book gets published. Do you have any idea how many rejection slips I've collected over the years?" No, I thought you wouldn't know. You never send anything out to publishers. "At least you don't know for certain that no one wants your work. I feel quite safe in saying that no one but the Oysters will ever see this book; that is, besides the editors who turn it down. And if by some fluke it does get published, well, I will have changed the names of the victims. And the suspects, I hope, will be equally difficult to recognize."

"Suspects? What suspects?" She looked positively ill.

"For god's sake, Joan, every murder story has suspects. Otherwise you have no story." There was a long pause while she sat with her hands over her face.

"Are you going to change the coloring of the boys from blond to brunet, and the setting to some place other than the University of Alaska campus?"

I looked at her in amazement.

"No. Why should I? Those details are integral to the story; at least they seem to be, at this point."

"But your book will call attention, by its very existence, to the fact that three blond freshmen died on the U of A campus."

"Joan, three blond boys did die, and no one seems to have paid any attention but me. So what are you worrying about?"

"Do you feel that there was something mysterious about the deaths of those boys?"

"Of course not. They are three deaths I just happened to pick out of a long list I got from the *Sourdough*. I am going to build my whole mystery around a great deal of coincidence. Although sometimes I think there is too much coincidence. Much too much." There was a long silence. I finished my tea.

"What are you going to do next?"

"Well, I want to see if there are any more coincidences in store for me. I think I'll visit the university and see if the victims were enrolled in the same course of study. But then, being freshmen, I suppose they were. I might just see if anyone there can remember them. I might even visit your husband."

I stood up.

"I have to go now. Thank you for the tea." I tried not to wince as I straightened my knee. "Joan, I don't think you're at all well. Are you coming down with something? Why don't you see your doctor?"

"It's not my health I'm worried about, Heather." Was there a slight emphasis on the "my"? I put on my raincoat, kissed Joan on the cheek, and walked stiffly out to my car.

I thought about her apartment as I drove away. It looked completely impersonal; I've seen hotel rooms that had more pictures and knickknacks.

When she left Philip Van Blarcom she'd left a whole life behind, and she'd made no effort to create a new life. I'd give anything to know what had happened between those two. What had he done? It couldn't have been a single reprehensible act. Lots of couples survive infidelity. It wasn't something that happened all of a sudden. I had seen her changing over the years, becoming more withdrawn, more quiet, as if nothing in life interested her anymore. I wondered that she was able to hold on to her job.

Enough tragedy. I should go home and attend to my knee, but I decided to call on the Williams sisters instead. That would cheer me up.

Chapter 15

What is human life but a comic strip?

As I headed toward the Williams sisters' home I couldn't help thinking how unusual they were, for identical twins. I suppose at one time they had been identical in appearance, but that was long before I knew them. Something must have happened to the metabolism of one or both; well, actually, Gwendolyn. Gwladys was as skinny as a rail, but Gwendolyn was obese almost to the point of being immobile.

They live in a small house off College Road. The yard is completely surrounded by metal fencing, and a neat little sign on the gate announces Kollege Kitty Kare. I rang, and Gwladys opened the door.

"Well, of all people! Heather! We were just talking about you! Weren't we, Gwendolyn? Let me take your raincoat. Are you ready for a cup of tea?" I wasn't. Not really. I still had a cup sloshing around inside and a scalded knee on the outside, but I lied.

The odor of cat urine was already assailing my nostrils. I noticed several litter boxes spotted handily around the sitting room. I hoped I wouldn't be a walking testimonial to Kollege Kitty Kare by the time I left. Gwendolyn was ensconced in an oversized recliner, tipped comfortably back. It had all kinds of knobs and cords, obviously some kind of automated rig. I suppose it gave her a thrust on the derriere whenever she wanted to disembark. Perhaps I would see a demonstration before I left. She was wearing a tent-like cotton dress, with two huge tomcats dozing on her midriff.

Gwladys, a little wren of a woman, flitted busily about. She hung up my raincoat and left to make tea. I sat down in an overstuffed chair, and a big white cat immediately leaped onto my lap and made himself comfortable on my black slacks. He dug his claws in like crampons and began to purr like a buzz saw. He had a bandage wrapped around his head.

"Hugo has an abscessed ear," explained Gwendolyn. She spoke in that deep, resonant tone common to many large people. "It has almost stopped draining, and hardly smells at all."

Maybe not from where she was sitting. She went on in some detail about his diagnosis, treatment, and diet until Gwladys showed up with the tea. I reached for the cup she held out to me, and I must have brushed against Hugo's sore ear. He gave a piercing shriek and lashed out with his paw, knocking the cup from my hand and spilling the contents into my lap. I let out a shriek too.

"Oh, poor baby," crooned Gwladys as she took him in her arms. "Him hurts so much. I so sorry. Mumsy will fix." And she carried the squalling beast out of the room. Gwendolyn catapulted out of her chair and waddled after her, while I sat there trying to pull my steaming slacks away from my thighs, hoping I didn't have third-degree burns. The only thing that kept me from being scalded to death was the thickness of the wool. Not that the sisters ever noticed. They eventually returned, Gwladys with a fresh cup of tea for me and Gwendolyn with assurances that she had given Hugo a sedative, and he was feeling no pain. Good for Hugo. That was more than I could say for myself.

I watched with interest as Gwendolyn backed into position, the robotic chair slowly lowered her, and the two tomcats reclaimed their pneumatic resting place. Gwladys handed her twin a cup of tea and settled down with her own.

"We were just talking about you and wondering how your book is coming along, weren't we, Gwendolyn?" Gwendolyn nodded. Oh? What had they been saying? I told them I'd been collecting information about the three victims, but I was still stymied for a motive.

"It's probably going to be the most difficult thing about the book. None of the three boys had been here long enough to have made enemies, or even very many friends."

"Perhaps it will be too difficult?" suggested Gwendolyn hopefully, in her stentorian tones.

"I don't think so. I'm going to stay with it."

"But Heather, a whole book! None of us have ever tackled anything so grandiose, have we, Gwladys?"

"I know you all think I'm crazy. I don't care. I'm going to do it." Why am I being so belligerent?

"But Heather, such a waste of time." Gwladys's turn. "And it's going to take forever. You shouldn't do this to yourself, should she, Gwendolyn?"

"Do what? What have I done for seventeen years but waste my time? I've got a whole file cabinet full of unpublished short stories and articles. There's room for one more." The two sisters exchanged a look of—forbearance? Complicity?

Gwendolyn: "What have you found out that's new?"

"Well, for one thing, the boys were all just beginning to look for part-time work when they died. If I could only find a prospective employer, or someone who knew them, it would be a great help to me." Once more, a look passing between the sisters made me feel I was missing something. Then, out of the corner of my eye, I saw that I was under siege. A huge rusty-colored tomcat was inching toward me on his belly. There was something ominous in his stealthy movement. His eyes never left mine. I waited for the sisters to intervene.

"Would you like another cup of tea?" asked Gwendolyn, in her resonating voice. My bladder said no. I wanted to visit their bathroom, but I was afraid to move. My attacker was getting closer and closer.

"It's Irish Breakfast tea," said Gwladys. "Being Welsh, we like a good strong tea. If we ever find a Welsh tea, of course we'll try it. Have you ever heard of Welsh breakfast tea, Heather?"

Just then my assailant pounced. He dug his claws into my right shin and gave a downward rake.

"Oh, naughty, naughty," said both sisters at once. The pain was excruciating. "Percy needs Time Out."

Gwladys gently extricated the feline from my leg, so as not to hurt him, deposited him in another room and closed the door. I could feel the blood running down my leg inside my slacks.

"You'd better have some more tea," purred Gladys, solicitously.

"No thanks. What I really need is your bathroom." As I followed Gwladys out of the room one of the cats left his perch on Gwendolyn's midriff and followed me. I tried to keep him out of the bathroom, but in so doing I closed the door on his tail. He let out loud screech. I gave up and let him in. As I struggled to loosen my clothing he made himself at home in a handy cat box. I had never used a bathroom in tandem before, especially not with a cat. As I hooked my garments he carefully raked over the contents of the box, then followed me out of the room.

"Feeling better?"

I was about to respond when I realized the question was addressed to the cat, whose tail now had a definite droop several inches from the tip. I thanked the twins for tea and put on my raincoat. My slacks were sticking to my lacerated leg, and my scalded thighs really smarted as I limped out to the car, but I managed to hoist myself painfully into the driver's seat and head home for some first aid treatment, like a tourniquet on my leg. I wondered if these visits to the Oysters were really necessary.

"Wow, Gram, what have *you* been up to?" Andrew let out a loud whistle as I staggered into the house. He filled a bucket with warm water and helped me soak my injured leg until I could remove my slacks. I related my adventures.

"I don't think much of *your* friends," commented Andrew. "Too rough."

The slacks were a lost cause; I'd never get the blood stains out, and Percy had left a good-sized tear. Oh well, easy come, easy go. I really wanted a long hot tub to heal my wounded spirit, but my wounded body said no.

I took a quick shower and emerged to find that Andrew had made a fire in the woodstove. He was willing to settle for grilled cheese sandwiches and soup, bless him, and later we watched some of Andrew's favorite TV shows. Not even assorted gunshots and screams could keep me awake. Eventually I made my way to bed, to dream all night that I was being attacked by snarling Oysters and fat and skinny cats.

The next morning was bright and sunny, so I knew I was doomed to spend a day at the lake. For some reason Andrew had failed to ask if CJ or Buzzie or Greaser might accompany us on the outing. Perhaps he already knew that they were not available. Anyway, it was just the two of us. That meant I got to help carry the canoe down the hill to the lake (keeping a second canoe at the lake cabin saves me a lot of hauling) and later, back up again. I got to paddle for two hours, instead of lolling back and taking it easy like the invalid I was.

One thing about Andrew, he has absolutely no respect for old age or infirmity. He never grabs my arm when we cross the street, or insists on carrying every little package. He treats me as an equal. He plays crude tricks on me and is not always perfectly respectful in his manner of address. It is almost possible to forget that I am a feeble old woman in his presence. Mostly it's rather refreshing.

As we paddled, Andrew kept up a patter that didn't seem to require my participation. I ruminated on the peculiar responses I was getting from the Oysters. Joan Van Blarcom's attitude toward my book was definitely hostile, and there was certainly something in the air besides cat at the Williams' menage. It wasn't encouragement, either. What had they been saying about me just before I arrived? Just as well I didn't know.

We sat for half an hour watching a young moose browsing at the edge of the lake. We examined the lodge of a beaver, who was returning home, his mouth gripping a sizeable chunk of alder, pointed at both ends where he had gnawed it from a felled tree. We heard the cry of a loon. As the hour grew late I suggested we head for home, but Andrew wanted to stay the night. I pleaded shortage of food; he pointed out that I kept canned goods, pancake mix, coffee, and powdered milk in the cabin, and he would catch fish for dinner.

He did: several fine trout. Sitting by the woodstove poring over my notes by the light of a gas lantern, I felt healed, even at peace.

Could Andrew have a therapeutic effect, or was it the lake? He was into his second book, *Treasure Island*, having collected his payment for the first. I turned in early, relieved to have aching muscles replacing the sting of burns and abrasions. We spent the next day much as the first, and then drove home in the late afternoon.

The following day was rainy, a real downpour. Andrew must be favored by the gods: the only two sunny days in the last two weeks, and we spent them at the lake.

I wanted a free afternoon so I could continue my visits to the Oysters. In a rare display of solicitude, Andrew offered to go with me to protect me from friends and cats, but I declined and sent him off to delight Buzzie's mother for the afternoon.

Abbie Buffmire and Marian Aldrich were next on my list, but neither was at home. Then I remembered it was Abbie's Garden Club day, and Marian was probably at the hospital, serving as a volunteer clerk in the gift shop like a good doctor's wife. I wondered if she had any problem with selling all those shiny new knick-knacks, given her dedication to recycling.

I decided to call on Florence Hokkainen, who lived up on Chena Ridge, fifteen minutes away. The rain fell steadily, and sometimes as I drove I felt a planing effect, as if the wheels were floating above the blacktop, but I managed to hold the road.

Chena Ridge is a choice place to live. For one thing, residents have a spectacular view of the Tanana Valley, with its two rivers, the Chena and the swifter Tanana into which it empties. Both are busy year round, with all kinds of boat traffic in summer and skiers, snowmachines, and dog teams in winter. The sparkling lights of Fairbanks brighten the long black winter night.

Many houses on the ridge cannot be seen from the road; some are situated on long driveways winding down the side of the hill, others appear to be perched precariously on outcroppings. Florence's house was one of these.

After a short wait I was rewarded by an answer to my knock. Florence greeted me warmly and then left to finish a phone call. I spent the interval studying Florence's decor: the furniture was ornate and gilded, the curtains heavy satin, the carpets thick and glossy.

What did it remind me of—maybe the interior of a sultan's harem? Or a—I won't say it. How would I know? I'd never been in one. She cut off my ruminations by returning with two cups of coffee and a large plateful of frosted cakes on a silver platter. She was so formally dressed I thought she must be about to leave for some state occasion, but she said no, she liked to look neat around the house. Every russet strand was carefully sprayed in place, every lacquered talon matched her crimson lips. Her amethyst necklace and earrings were probably real; I know the diamond rings were. Her purple satin dress was beaded.

When I first arrived in Fairbanks, I used to see young women who looked like Florence in the beauty parlor. I gathered they had standing appointments for the same time every afternoon. Elaborately dressed, their bright-colored hair piled in layers of curls, thick make-up on their faces, they were very friendly and outgoing and I enjoyed talking to them. Later a friend warned me, in a loud whisper, not to speak to them, and after that they ignored me.

I noted with satisfaction a muscular young fellow on the porch washing storm windows. Florence always had a male or two around the place to do her chores, and she liked them young. I wondered whether I couldn't make something of that.

"Sweetie, tell Florence about your book." From her manner you'd think she'd said, "Tell Florence about your love life," but I suppose that intimate manner gets to be a habit, in the catering business. I cleared my throat.

"Well, there's not much to tell. I'm still collecting information about my three victims. You know, the college students." She nodded.

"Are you still going to use Fairbanks for your setting?" My turn to nod.

"What about your suspects?" Good god, another expert on mystery writing. Had I used those terms in speaking to all of the Oysters, or were they having consultations about my book and passing the vocabulary around?

"Actually, I've decided..." I turned coward: "to postpone deciding on the suspects for a little while. Until I have a motive. And that seems to be the toughest part of writing this book."

"Oh? Florence wonders if you haven't bitten off more than you can chew. Why not go back to writing those wonderful little short stories we all admire so much? They are always so successful."

"Successful! I've had three published out of a bushel. And most likely this won't get published, either. I regard it as a challenge, a mental exercise. If Socrates could learn to play the fidibus in his old age, I can write a mystery. For myself. And for the Oysters. "

"Socrates? Do I know him? No? Don't do it for the Oysters, honey. Florence thinks most of them would prefer that you just abandon the whole idea."

"How does Florence know? Has she taken a poll?" I was beginning to feel decidedly testy. I was also losing my taste for Oysters.

"There has been talk," she admitted, darkly. "Florence thinks you should let those dead boys rest in peace. And so does everybody else."

"Florence," I said, wearily, " I'm going to finish this book. I'm going to finish this book if it kills me." The words had a familiar ring. Where had I heard them lately? I asked for my raincoat. She left and came back with a bottle of brandy and two snifters.

"Now don't rush off mad, honey. Florence and Heather have been friends for too long to let a little old book come between them. Florence didn't mean to hurt your feelings. Let Florence pour you a little brandy and we'll forget about the old book."

Well, I had one small brandy, and we talked quietly for a few minutes. If she thought things were all smoothed over when I left, she was wrong. I was still seething.

❋ ❋ ❋ ❋ ❋ ❋

The rain was pounding down. Visibility was very poor as I drove up her steep driveway. I was barely out onto the highway and just starting to accelerate when a speeding pickup truck blasted his horn and passed so close he nearly sideswiped my car. I braked, lost control, and planed right off the road. The car broke through the metal guard rail and rolled down the hill. It seemed as if it rolled over several times. I thought it would never stop rolling. I hung in the air while the car rocked back and forth, and then rolling over one more time, came to rest on its front end against a great spruce tree. I was wearing my seatbelt, and I suppose that, and the tree, were all that saved my life.

Dizzy and disoriented—for god's sake, alliteration at a time like this?—I sat still; rather, I hung still, until my head cleared. I carefully tested various appendages; nothing seemed broken or bleeding. Afraid to move, even if I could, for fear of jiggling the car and disturbing its precarious balance, and having nothing better to do, I lapsed into unconsciousness. I don't know how long I was out. I remember a bright light, and voices.

"They're probably dead," said one, cheerfully.

I moved an arm.

"Look, there's movement! Someone's still alive!"

I was very much alive, and I was freezing cold. Then the voice came from right outside the car.

"Can you hear me?"

I moved my arm again. The upshot was that I lay—no, I wasn't lying, I was hanging from the seat back—until an hour later, when two policemen helped me out of the car and up the hill, and the wrecked car followed suit at the end of a long tow line. Then, dammit, one of the policemen smelled the brandy and gave me a breathalizer test. I was never so angry in my whole life. Of course I passed the test, but I got a citation for Basic Speed, the rationale being that I'd had the accident, ergo I must have done something wrong. They wanted to take me to the hospital, but I insisted on going home. Rowe was waiting at my door.

"Drunk again!" he said, before the policeman or I could get a word in. The copper protested, too much, and finally things were straightened out. Rowe apologized for his untimely humor. I tried to explain to him what had happened. Then, after a hot shower, I crawled under my down comforter and passed out again.

I slept the night through. Rowe was still asleep on the couch when I came to. I was bruises from head to foot; in fact, there was very little of me that wasn't scalded, scratched, or bruised. I hurt when I moved, so I didn't. Rowe fixed us bacon and eggs when he woke up. Apparently my car had been spotted about a half-hour after I left Florence's house; a passing motorist saw the bent guardrail and stopped to look down the hill. He immediately called the police, so I had been saved from possible hypothermia and goodness knows what else. I used to think I was pretty rugged, but not any more.

Once he was assured that I would live, Rowe went off to work. I made the morning news. Heather Adams, mystery writer, in a one-car accident on Chena Ridge. Oh well. I switched off the phone and went back to bed.

Chapter 16

But life can be very complicated even if you stay home?

Two weeks later I still wasn't feeling like myself. My body was a mass of black and blue bruises, my ribs were sore, I was dizzy when I stood up, and I hurt when I lay down. I couldn't think clearly, and after that chilling time in the car I thought I'd never be warm again. I spent most of the time under my down quilt. Like royalty of old, I even entertained from under the quilt: Oysters, neighbors, Unitarians, and retired teachers came in for a chat (they wanted the real lowdown) and a cup of tea.

Andrew made the tea; in fact, he assumed charge of the household. My meals consisted of charred cheese sandwiches and canned soup. My young butler greeted visitors with a newfound charm, relieving them of their contributions, and letting them know in subtle ways (for Andrew) when he thought they had stayed long enough.

We played cribbage, gin rummy, Boggle, Scrabble, and, of course, poker. My grandson was not averse to separating an aging, infirm, crippled invalid from her ready cash.

Dennis Wheeler put me through a kind of third degree.

"So, Heather, tell me exactly what happened, " he ordered sternly.

"You know what happened. Someone in a pickup forced me off the road."

"Did you see the driver?"

"Of course not. It was raining too hard."

"And you hadn't had anything to drink?"

"I had a shot glass of brandy. Nothing else. Ask Florence Hokkainen."

He stood there rubbing his chin. "So you planed off the road. What do you mean by *planed*?"

"Dammit, Dennis, don't patronize me! I've been driving in blizzards, rainstorms, hail storms, and sixty below zero, since before you were born! I know planing when I feel it. It's as if you're flying, skimming. You don't feel contact with the road. So, has Raysheen made lieutenant yet?"

That was unkind. Raysheen had made sergeant soon after he did. She'd better not beat him to lieutenant. He turned and walked out of the room. Good. Someone tries to kill me and I get blamed.

What did I just say? I could hear it echoing in my head, even though I hadn't spoken aloud. I really do feel as if someone tried to kill me. Had the murderer I created become real, or had he been real all along? Once again I wondered, if I tear up my notes, will he go away? But my imaginary killer didn't know about my notes. Only the Oysters knew about them, and a more harmless bunch of women never existed. Perhaps one of them is innocently passing information to a not-so-innocent friend. Perhaps I'm becoming paranoid. If someone is out to get you, you're not paranoid. But the driver who ran me off the road may not have been out to get me. God, am I confused.

Andrew stayed for two more weeks and then had to leave to get ready for school, but by then I was able to spare him. He returned every afternoon to dispose of edible donations, with Popsie's help.

Eventually, as physical activity became less painful, I started working over my long-neglected house, a bit here, a bit there. I had the furnace winterized. I got Andrew to put yard furniture, tools, and the lawn tractor in the shed. I did the paperwork for the car insurance; I dusted; I put things away; I did everything but work on my book. And I deliberately missed the first meeting of the Oysters in late September. I turned down the suggestion that we have the September meeting here, even though my house was spic and span, and I refused offers to pick me up.

I even did a little reading, mysteries, mostly. I am now a much better critic than I used to be. For example, I think that often the stories are great: the characters, plot, and suspense are fine, until you get to the unraveling. After the buildup to the moment when the murderer is revealed, the story plummets. Well, of course it does. It's supposed to plummet. What I mean is, the murderer, who has been intelligent enough to lead the best of Scotland Yard on a merry chase for weeks, months, if not years turns out to have risked his future, his very life, for some trivial reason, and the *modus operandi* is often so complicated that I can hardly understand it.

Somewhere along the line I began to mull over my book. And then I sat down and wrote three whole chapters. I knew then that I was going to finish this book, whether or not it ever got published. Well, I knew it wouldn't be published.

Rowe, who was conspicuous by his attentiveness, dropped in almost every day. I could read his mind; he thought I was getting too old and senile to be living on my own, that I would soon be moving to the Pioneer Home, where aging Alaskans spend their last days in custodial comfort. I could see he didn't buy my story that someone had run me off the road.

Some damned fool had apparently spread the story that I had been drinking, and that was why I'd had the accident. I might never have known if Florence hadn't phoned to reassure me.

"Florence is scotching the rumors," she said, in her inimitable way. "Florence has phoned *everyone* to tell them that you only had one teeny little brandy, and you positively were not drunk."

"Thank you, Florence," I said, weakly.

I bought a new car, since mine had been totaled. I simply had the dealer deliver the newest model of my old station wagon. I felt pretty good, but my spirit was still dampened. A person can take only so much humiliation. Christopher Morley said that no mature woman is ever embarrassed. What did he know?

Suddenly it was October. Repenting a little of my recent churlishness, I agreed to let the Oysters have the Halloween Eve meeting at my house. I think every single Oyster phoned to say she appreciated my generosity. I was beginning to take the Oysters with a grain of salt, but I was glad to patch things up.

Although I was still rather inactive, the next couple of weeks were a time of great literary achievement. I'm joking. But I did get three more chapters written. I managed to introduce the idea of the kind of murderer I was looking for, combining the profile I had worked out during my Vermont trip with the Adams theory, which you'll find in Chapter 10, if you want to refresh your memory.

❋ ❋ ❋ ❋ ❋ ❋

Josephine Tey, author of *The Daughter of Time*, says: "Your true criminal has two unvarying characteristics, and it is these two characteristics which make him a criminal. Monstrous vanity and colossal selfishness."

Whatever motivation I ultimately came up with, monstrous vanity and colossal selfishness would have to be a part.

I also brought out the coincidences I had turned up in the backgrounds of the three victims and their parents: the fact that all three had been born on Eielson Air Force Base, that all three fathers were officers, that all three victims were tall and blond, with a strong resemblance to one another. They were all outstanding students with a scientific bent and very good athletes. All were looking for part-time work. I felt that I finally had the framework of my mystery, and by the December meeting, with a little luck, I should be able to come up with a fully realized murderer. I just noticed that I am beginning to refer to the three boys as *victims*. I guess that's a step in the right direction. What about the murderer: is he real, or isn't he?

Having the meeting at my house made me feel that I had rejoined the world of the living. As usual in late October, the temperature was a frosty –25, there was a light layer of snow, and several Oysters mentioned as they came in that the northern lights were out. I had been too busy to notice, so I threw on a jacket and we spent a few minutes enjoying the ghostly display. Great ribbons of pastel reds and greens and every combination thereof waved to and fro across the night sky. Sometimes, when I ask myself, "Why am I here?" I forget to include the aurora as one of the reasons.

Everyone was on time. Much to my surprise, even Gwendolyn Williams showed up. I hadn't seen her since the afternoon of the tea party at their house. I remembered Marian Aldrich's prudence and guided her toward a suitable chair. In the past Gwendolyn had distinguished herself mainly by her absence, but now she was becoming a regular.

We quickly demolished the cheesecake and Sanka and got down to business. Gwendolyn had actually done some writing, a lengthy piece on the evolution of the cat, starting back with the blob. It was thorough and scholarly, and she read it in her usual sonorous tones, which gained in volume what they lost in velocity. Gwladys had done the research, the legwork, so it was a joint effort.

Florence Hokkainen, after all this time, still hadn't reached Anchorage. She stalled with more detailed descriptions of people, roadhouses, clothing, scenery, meals, and weather. She even had an itemized expense account and an evil glint in her eye.

Abbie Buffmire's *Son of Gardening in the North* was aimed at the journeyman gardener rather than the rank beginner. This time she went into some detail for those who want to get into worms: care and feeding, housing, breeding. She was followed by Katie George who had several new chapters of *Daughter of the Yukon*, devoted to a childhood summer spent at a family fish camp on the river. It was extraordinarily good, and I said so. The others agreed.

The meeting was longer than usual. Joan Van Blarcom had her second story about the little girl and her dog team; this time the little girl's team won. And of course Marcia Wayman had another love poem. Poor Marcia.

Marian Aldrich had an essay on the importance of recycling if we are to save the planet. Abbie and I suggested she write a book entitled *The Joy of Recycling*. She said she would think about it. Then, finally, it was my turn.

Did I imagine it, or was there a feeling of tension as I passed out three copies of the first chapter? Or was it suspense? If it was suspense, it boded well for my book. As each page was read, it was passed on, and soon everyone was reading and taking notes. Late as it was, they insisted on reading all six chapters. I'd thought three would be enough, but I was delighted. Then came the comments.

Marian: "That is a very sad story. I never cried over a mystery before."

Me: "Oh, dear. I must check my rule book and see if that's permissible."

Florence: "How will you explain the way the boys resemble each other? Florence thinks that's rather weird. Did you make that up?"

Me: "No. So far I haven't made anything up."

Katie: "I wonder why no one else ever noticed the resemblance."

Me: "Maybe because, the cases not being connected in any way, they were handled by three different policemen."

Marcia: "How would you know that?"

Me: "Let's just say I'm becoming an expert on these three deaths."

Joan Van Blarcom stood up with a tissue over her mouth and left the room. In a few minutes she reappeared and apologized. She thought she was coming down with something. I suggested she not stay for the full meeting, but she wouldn't leave. We resumed.

Abbie: "Why don't you skip all the detective work and just write the book? You can make it come out any way you like."

Me: "I just don't have the imagination. I need all the information I can get. I think I've stumbled onto something really good, so I'm going to stay with it."

Gwladys: "Have you decided on a title?"

Me: "Not yet. Maybe one of you has an idea."

Marcia: "How about *The Case of the Frozen Freshmen*?" And she laughed. I was furious.

"There's nothing funny about the death of three young boys," I snapped.

Marcia apologized.

Abbie: "Do you know more than you've told in these six chapters?"

Me: "Lots more, but you'll have to wait for the next installment."

Florence: "Florence doesn't understand how research is going to help you. Those boys didn't even know one another, and they weren't murdered."

Me: "I don't know."

Gwladys: "Who are you going to use for your suspects?" Long pause. "Are you thinking of using the Oysters?"

Well, all hell broke loose. They tied Gwladys' question to my recent unannounced visits, and it was quite a while before I had everyone calmed down. I lied. I said I had no idea, never had had any idea, of turning any Oysters into murderers. I don't think they believed me. They were one bunch of angry Oysters as they took their leave. No one offered to stay behind to help me tidy up, which suited me fine. I was as angry as they were. I drank the last coffee in the pot, rinsed the cups, and that's all I remember.

❄ ❄ ❄ ❄ ❄ ❄

Andrew, it seems, saved my life. He wanted to go trick-or-treating the next night, Halloween, and he needed an adult chaperone, as both Rowe and Alice had meetings to attend. So he phoned and phoned. At ten, unable to sleep until he had his problem resolved, he complained to his father that I was not answering my phone. I had mentioned to Rowe that I was hosting the Oysters, and he knew that they always break up early. He told Andrew I was probably in the tub, with the phone switched off. Then he gave Marian Aldrich a call to see if I had gone out for a drink with anyone. Highly unlikely, but possible. She assured him I was busy cleaning up when she left.

At eleven he jumped in his car and came to see for himself, and found me unconscious in my bedroom. I was wearing my nightgown, and was apparently about to climb into bed when I collapsed on the floor. He was unable to revive me, so he called an ambulance. I had ingested a potentially lethal dose of chloral hydrate.

When I woke up in the hospital, my son was sitting at my bedside looking exhausted. He stared at me for a while, and then said wryly, "That was a stupid thing to do, Mother."

"What was?" I asked, groggily.

"You know what I mean. Since when do you take sleeping pills?"

"I never touch the things."

"Look, Ma, you don't have to kid me. You took a whole bunch of sleeping pills in your coffee last night."

"I did not. Why should I lie?"

"I don't know, Ma. I always thought you were one sharp old girl. Now, in six weeks' time you've driven your car off the road and overdosed yourself with sleeping pills."

"I didn't. I can't explain it, but I didn't take them. You forgot to say I got drunk and ..."

"Don't quibble, Ma. I know you weren't drinking. But something is rotten in Denmark. If you didn't put the chloral hydrate in your coffee, who did? Are any of the Oysters turning into vicious killers?" He smiled at the absurdity of it. "Have you been making any enemies lately?"

"No more than usual. There must be a perfectly reasonable explanation."

"Are you sure one of the Oysters isn't getting tired of your stories?"

Just then the nurse came in to cut his visit short, and he went home for some much-needed rest. I dropped off and dreamed that the huge doors of the Pioneer Home opened up and swallowed me. Whole.

Chapter 17

*The mind, a secret little drugstore, likes to
compound its own little prescriptions.*

I did not take any sleeping pills. *I don't have any sleeping pills in the house.* But I don't think anyone believed me. Certainly not Rowe. I felt like having a tantrum and screaming "I didn't do it, I didn't do it, I didn't do it," to all and sundry. But no one would believe me, anymore than they believed that I hadn't been drinking when I drove off the road.

I thought about the evening of my "overdose." I remembered perfectly well taking the oversize coffeepot out for the occasion. I keep it on a high shelf in a closet in the kitchen, and I have to lift it down very carefully or it will fall on my head. I washed and dried it, and placed it on the stove. Absolutely clean. There couldn't have been anything in the coffee I served the Oysters, or the meeting would have turned into one big slumber party. I remembered every single move I made, including pouring the last bit of coffee into my cup and drinking it. I remembered rinsing the cups and the coffee pot and putting them away. I didn't remember feeling sick, or drowsy. I didn't remember getting into my nightgown.

If the experts are sure that the drug was in my coffee, I suppose it must have been there. I only know I didn't put it there. And if I didn't, who did? The chloral hydrate must have found its way into my coffeepot some time between the last cup I poured for an Oyster and the general departure. It had to be that way.

One could say that the inbred frugality of my Scottish forbears, plus the lasting effects of growing up during the Depression, were my undoing. I never throw anything out, not even the stale dregs left in an almost empty coffeepot. Any of the Oysters could have predicted what I would do. Perhaps one of them was in a prankish mood? I have not been aware that we had any practical jokers in the group, except possibly myself, and then on only that rare and fortuitous occasion when it would be criminal to ignore a perfect set-up. But that night, me alone with an almost empty coffeepot was not a situation begging for action. Only someone terribly naive about drugs and with a perverse sense of humor would have set me up for that near-brush with eternity.

I sometimes suspected Florence of deliberately badgering us with the annoyingly slow progress of her biography. She knows we're all waiting to know had she or had she not been a hooker? Will she really ever tell? She often has a wicked twinkle in her eye as she forces us to read pages of trivia while we stifle our curiosity and our impatience. And Marcia has a habit of making totally uncalled-for remarks. But they usually aren't funny, except to her. I don't know. I just don't know. But until I do, I'm going to be wary of Oysters.

Have you ever noticed that detectives in mystery novels lead lives totally circumscribed by murder? I mean, they live for murder; everything else goes down before it. They don't have to deal with a lot of extraneous matter on a daily basis. The corpse appears, and boom! They are off on the chase, like the bloodhounds that they are. While I, on the other hand, have continually to fight my way free of all kinds of impedimenta, such as grandsons and parents and college roommates and a creeping tendency to be accident prone.

So here I am, recuperating again, not from a cold, not from the flu, nor from bursitis, rheumatism, or anything else even slightly respectable but from a damned overdose of sleeping pills, which I swear I never took. And of course last month I drove off the road, wrecking both my car and myself, and I know there were, and still are, rumors that I was drunk. On top of all that, I'm getting paranoid. I keep imagining that Rowe and Alice, and even Andrew, think that I am no longer capable of managing my own life. Andrew has offered several times to move in with me, and while I know that part of the reason is the impending birth of the new baby, I'm sure he must hear his parents talking about me. "Mother is failing rapidly. We must do something about her," and all that sort of thing.

I think Andrew is trying, in his way, to take care of me. I imagine pity and, at the very least, speculation in every look, everywhere I go. Kindnesses that I would once have accepted gladly, to be returned "farther on down the road," I now regard as charitable offerings to a senile old woman. I see a new softness, a gentleness, in every look, every word, as if I have suddenly become very fragile. When was the last time Rowe insulted me, or Andrew tried to involve me in some shady deal? I can't even remember.

I left the hospital after forty-eight hours and then lolled around the house for a week, once again inundated by stinking flowers, disgusting puddings, and unsavory broths. Not even Andrew or Popsie could stomach them.

I tried to build up my strength by taking short and then longer walks, but the temperature now, in early November, was getting down to minus twenty-five and colder every day. Not really cold, but I couldn't help feeling that if I so much as slipped and turned my ankle, I could end up in the Pioneer Home. I had been spared the trick-or-treating with Andrew, although I'd have preferred the trick-or-treating to what actually happened. Buzzie's father had accompanied the boys. I began to long for the old days when I was forced to go on canoe trips and school outings and even X-rated film parties.

I returned to my aquasize class. I hadn't attended since I started the book. My classmates greeted me too enthusiastically, like a long-lost sinner returning to the fold. I felt condescension and pity. I didn't go back. Then I got something of a reprieve.

My daughter-in-law, now in the last stages of her pregnancy, asked me if I would accompany Andrew's hockey team to Anchorage for a tournament, with a side trip to Gilhooly. It would be a good rest for me (who was she kidding?), they were all very good boys (ditto), and there would be other parents along, of course. Andrew added his two cents.

"The guys all want you to go, Gram, and besides, all you do is sit around the house all day doing nothing. You might as well have some fun." The implied criticism delighted me and suddenly I felt very good, as if Andrew were setting me up for one of his nefarious schemes, and so I gratefully said yes.

The boys would be leaving in a week. That gave me time to move in the young housesitting lovers, arrange to board Popsie, and pull out my cold weather gear. I even had a few days to do some work around the house. My recent flirtations with mortality reminded me that should my next flirtation turn out to be a more permanent affair, someone, probably Alice, would be going through my personal belongings. I decided to clean house for Alice.

I began by sorting through all my underwear. This took quite a long time, because my Scottish genes kicked in, and I kept lowering my standards, rescuing more and more, until I finally said, "To hell with it," and threw the whole works out. Then I sorted through bureau drawers, shoes, and seasonal clothing. We older people tend to hang on to too much, too long. I amassed quite a few garbage bags of good stuff for the thrift store and even emptied my piggy bank and rolled the coins. When I finally quit, I felt that should my strange tendency toward self-immolation proceed to its logical conclusion, Alice would be making far fewer sniffs of disapproval as she sorted through my effects.

Anchorage, our nearest city of any size (we have only three: Anchorage, Fairbanks, and Juneau, in that order), is almost four hundred miles away. A trip by bus requires about as much gear as an expedition to the South Pole; a trip to the North Pole wouldn't be that big a deal. Buses occasionally break down and finding spare parts invariably takes hours; they usually send to the factory in Michigan. Or so it seems. For the trip to Gilhooly and Anchorage I packed a goose-down sleeping bag, my minus-fifty-degree down parka, insulated boots and mittens, wool slacks, sweaters, hat—complete emergency gear.

We left for Anchorage at six a.m. on November 20. We had a new-looking Greyhound-type bus. Looks don't fool me anymore. I've almost frozen to death in too many fancy new buses. The boys were sleepy and quiet for the first hour or so. The second hour they broke into their snacks, which were supposed to last all the way to Anchorage. In the third hour Buzzie threw up, and we had to stop in Big Delta to clean the bus. Also the boys needed a pit stop, which they did about every fifty miles for the rest of the trip.

We reached Gilhooly in midafternoon. A small village of several hundred inhabitants, every Christmas Gilhooly sends teams to Fairbanks for the hockey tournaments. The Gilhooligans rent a couple of buses, and the whole village goes along: every grandmother, every infant. Their arrival in Fairbanks creates a stir far out of proportion to their importance in the tournament. Fairbanks boys say Gilhooligans cheat, and point to supposedly twelve-year-old players who obviously shave, male players on female teams, and vice versa. However they do it, they manage to field several teams in various age levels who play extremely fierce (i.e., dirty) hockey. Gilhooligan babies never seemed to cry, but their grandmothers could out-scream and out-swear any fans I've ever seen anywhere.

There were several dozen small wooden houses, a little store, and a small school building that included space for the teachers to live, all centered around the outdoor hockey rink. The best building in town was probably the warm-up shack, which was next to the school building in size. It probably served as the town hall as well.

Each side fielded only two teams for this little contest. CJ pointed to a boy who had just played for a twelve-year-old, or "Squirt" team. He was suckling his baby over in the bleachers. Our boys wrapped up the games quickly and we left, amid mutual hard feelings and name calling, as usual.

As well as our Fairbanks boys, Anchorage was hosting teams from Wasilla, Palmer, Kenai, Soldotna, Eagle River, Anchor Point, and Homer. The boys were parceled out in pairs to various players' homes. I overheard the coaches matching up the boys, and I was mortified, when they came to Andrew's name, to hear, "Andrew and CJ—no. Andrew and Buzzie—no. Andrew and Greaser—no," and so on down the list.

Andrew finally found his match in Benjamin, a gentleman and scholar and all-around exemplary character. The second night in

Anchorage they were split up, and Andrew was taken in tow by one of the coaches. Benjamin received the first reprimand of his blameless career, but not the last; he was forever afterwards a force to reckon with and also one of Andrew's best friends. I hadn't seen or heard Benjamin on the trip down, but he was quite visible and audible on the way home.

I stayed in a hotel near the rink and walked over to the games. The host families were responsible for the boys, thank heaven, as I now needed a rest from the rest cure. Andrew's team placed second in the tournament. Immediately after the last game we piled into the bus and left for home; but strangely, I felt a kind of reluctance as we headed north. I wasn't as eager to end this trip and get back to my home as I should have been, because all of a sudden, I had a feeling that someone wanted me dead, and I was afraid.

We chaparones had hoped the boys would sleep on the way home, but no such luck. Instead, they gathered in the back of the bus and played cards.

I was mulling over this new sensation, the sensation of being "the hunted," when two mothers informed me that Andrew was relieving all the boys of their pocket money, and besides, gambling was immoral. I pulled Andrew out of the game, and he spent the rest of the trip dozing beside me. His only comment was "Don't feel bad, Gram. They didn't have enough money left to make it worth my while anyhow." But it was worth my while. His presence was strangely comforting.

Chapter 18

All that is left to me, I said, hoping for inspired contradiction,
is Surrender. I was ready to admit defeat…

The hockey trip had definitely cleared my head, and I was raring to get back to my writing. I paid off the young lovers, picked up Popsie from the kennel, and despite the fact that I had been traveling all night, sat down at my desk.

I had to give myself the usual synopsis. I have wasted more time reviewing my notes after these long hiatuses—that sounds like a word that should have a nice Latin plural, but I haven't been able to find it. The Romans apparently never had to contend with more than one hiatus at a time. (If I were ever to be reincarnated, and mind you, I don't believe in reincarnation, I will study Latin next time around.)

I had the setting—Fairbanks, of course; the closed society would continue to be my dear friends, the Oysters, dammit, but what could I say about them? I pecked away for a while, transcribing the odd behaviors I had witnessed. No, *experienced*. Were the Oysters some sort of deadly group of child murderers? After all these years, didn't I know them at all?

I had to get away from them. I moved on to the motive. I didn't have a motive. I couldn't think of one. I couldn't imagine why anyone would kill those boys. I gave up. I couldn't write.

In the past I've always found the best thing to do when hit with writer's block is just keep writing. The very process of kicking out whatever shows up seems to rouse the subconscious mind. A lot of creative types—writers, artists, musicians—have written about their ability to use their subconscious minds at will. For example, Frank Lloyd Wright would put the stalled project "on the back burner," and his subconscious would continue working on that project while with his conscious mind he tackled something else. Eventually the solution to the first project would just pop into his mind. Many people in fields that demand a great deal of creativity have their own ways of tapping their subconscious minds.

Hoping my subconscious mind had taken the hint, I moved back to the Oysters. We seem to be speaking again. I had been ready to split the sheets after that last meeting, but my near fatal mishap had brought them all rushing to my bedside. I had rather mixed feelings about them now. If I didn't put the chloral hydrate in the coffee, one of them did. Why? Must I spend the rest of my life worrying about which Oyster is trying to do me in? Perhaps I should just resign. I'd thought about it often enough.

If I couldn't write, I could plan. So what should I do next? Well, I hadn't completed my home visits to the Oysters. I didn't know if I was ready for all the physical abuse those visits seemed to entail. Especially if one of them was out to get me. Sometimes I felt as if they were all out to get me.

Maybe they won't even let me in the door. They're definitely aroused about something. I'd really expected them to be pleased to find themselves characters in my book. Maybe I'm not the only Oyster to be troubled with creeping senility; maybe there's an epidemic.

I decided that I could visit Katie George and Abbie Buffmire without danger to life and limb. Katie's only drawback is that dozens of relatives in the villages call her place home when they're in town, so a quiet cup of tea with her might be out of the question. And at Abbie's, while there are sprinklers and coils of hose and piles of noxious, decaying substances to trip up the unwary in the summer, a winter visit should be pretty safe. The whole idea is to keep moving. I didn't have a lot of time, because Thanksgiving was next week, and I was hosting the family. Alice loves to have Thanksgiving dinner at their house, but with a baby coming next month she was in no condition to take on that much work. I would borrow Andrew to help get ready and to clean up afterward, thus relieving myself of any leftovers problem. I decided to look in on Katie, without any great expectations, and Abbie afterwards.

Katie owns a little house on Ballaine Road. She and her ex-husband used to live in a large house on the river until her very sudden departure two years ago, right around the time Joan left Philip. I wonder why two Oysters left their spouses at approximately the same time? Unlike Katie, though, Joan never left the Oysters; sometimes I feel that for her, we have provided a little bit of stability to someone who'd suffered great loss.

Katie had owned the little house on Ballaine Road before she married Mr.—I can't remember his name—it was her second marriage. She moved in with a grown daughter until she could get the tenants out of her house.

Katie was home and she had a houseful of company, but she got me inside the house and my coat off before I could offer my lame excuse for not staying. As she put my coat away I observed that her house was full of all kinds of Alaska artifacts and keepsakes: beaded slippers, beautiful baskets, and walls covered with paintings and drawings. Pieces of wolf skins were draped over the backs of chairs, and four middle-aged female cousins were working together on what appeared to be a tribal chief's ceremonial winter costume, like the beautiful outfits that show up at the dog races during Winter Carnival, in March.

A meat stew was simmering in the kitchen. My sense of smell wasn't acute enough to determine whether it was moose or caribou, but it smelled good. Katie said it was moose and invited me to stay and have some, but I told her I had another appointment, which was only a half-lie. She introduced me to her cousins, who were traditional Indian women: dark skin, long black hair braided or worn in a ponytail, medium height, not quite as slim as Katie.

While Katie made tea—she said it was time for a break—her cousins demonstrated how the outfit would go together. The hooded tunic of moose hide and the matching trousers would have fur and beaded trim when they were finished.

Katie never mentioned my book; her mind was clearly occupied with other things, certainly not dead blond boys or fear that I would make her a murder suspect in my book. So she was probably the one who doped my coffee. Anyway, I almost hated to leave as I walked out of her house on my hind feet, unscalded and unscratched. If I smelled of anything, it was moose stew. How refreshing.

Andrew had been complaining about my old snow shovel, so I decided to take a roundabout route to Abbie's and pick up a new one at Aurora Lumber. As I crossed the Wendell Street bridge I noted that the city snow dump was well under way. The snow dump is where the trucks deposit snow plowed off the city streets all winter. In really snowy years it can reach several stories in height. Come spring breakup, city bulldozers push the snow into the river. I always worry that some child will climb up on it when the snow is rotting and simply disappear. Like Bill.

Like Bill! So that's where he spent the time he was missing, in that mountain of rotting snow and ice! I knew it! I knew it! I almost stopped the car in the middle of the bridge; I caught myself just in time. I was so excited that I wanted to turn the car around and go somewhere and do something. But what? I managed to persuade myself that there was no place I should go, and nothing I could do at that very moment with my new information, for information it was, I felt certain. I breathed a sigh of thanks to my faithful subconscious mind; that hadn't taken long at all. I decided to go on to Abbie's. But first I stopped at Aurora Lumber and bought the snow shovel.

Abbie's famous gardens keep her busy in the summer. She winters over a tub of worms, which eat her vegetable and fruit trimmings, and a large goldfish named Arthur, who resides in a garbage can all winter and in a rocky pool in the summer. She prides herself on being almost totally self-sufficient and on not using more than her fair share of the planet's resources, so it's not surprising that her other consuming interest is recycling.

Abbie doesn't travel much, not even to escape the extremes of January and February. She says she can't trust anyone else to care for Arthur the goldfish and the worms, and indeed, the only time I have ever seen her angry was when some housesitters let the worms starve to death. It must have been a problem of aesthetics, because Arthur the goldfish survived. Anyway, Abbie catches up on indoor work once her fall harvest is in.

She must be in her midsixties, probably the mean age for Oysters. She is long widowed; I never knew her husband. I heard one Oyster suggest that Abbie shredded and composted the late Mr. Buffmire, which is absolute nonsense. Abbie has told us over and over never to feed protein matter to our worms, only vegetable and fruit trimmings.

Abbie is the only one of the Oysters to have had a book published. Some might say that the fact that she published it herself detracts somewhat from the honor of being published, but her book certainly is a best seller, in Fairbanks. Abbie would never make a good suspect, because if she wouldn't murder someone over the death of her worms, she wouldn't murder at all. So what was I doing here?

I knocked on the door, and Abbie immediately yelled something back. I thought she said "Come in!" but she must have said "Coming!" because I pushed the door open and there was a great crash. Abbie was painting the vestibule ceiling. Fortunately she was only halfway up the ladder, so she wasn't hurt, but I had a small dent in my head from a bucket of paint. After I had rinsed most of the paint out of my hair and put on some generously sized clothing from Abbie's recycling bag—mine were soaking in her washing machine—we had a nice cup of tea. We discussed our various writing projects, and Abbie asked why I didn't switch to biography or a historical novel. I told her I would think about one or the other for my *next* writing project, after I finish my mystery. Having done her duty, she dropped the subject, and we had a pleasant visit. I'm not sure I learned anything. I already knew Oysters could be dangerous.

Chapter 19

You don't need to stir from your place,
whatever it is. Just sit there and watch.

I had missed some of the white paint in my hair. It hardened, and short of cutting it all off there wasn't much I could do. The only good thing: the paint was not oil-based, so sooner or later it would flake out. If I massaged and brushed violently I could probably speed the process. I didn't want to have to go around explaining that I'd had another accident or wear a wig or a turban to avoid explanations. Discretion seemed to dictate that I avoid the Oysters for a few days, and anyway, preparing for Thanksgiving would limit my social life.

As I cut and chopped and minced I did a lot of thinking about what to do next on the mystery. I decided to complete my visits to the two remaining Oysters on Friday, the day after Thanksgiving, assuming my hair was restored to its usual brindle color; then I'd do some research at the university.

The temperature dropped to thirty degrees below zero the day before Thanksgiving. Mention minus thirty down in the states and people think you're crazy to be living here. People can freeze to death at minus thirty degrees. They freeze to death at plus thirty degrees in the states. But minus thirty isn't cold as winter temperatures go; it's only cold the first time it hits, in October or November. By January or February we think minus thirty is balmy. You'd have to live through a spell of minus fifty, or colder, to understand what a relief minus thirty can be.

The first cold temperatures seem to take a lot of us by surprise. Don't ask me why: they arrive right on schedule every year. Some people never think of winterizing their cars or their furnaces until the cold hits. Consequently, automobile mechanics and furnace repairmen are swamped during the first cold spells. Auto body people, on the other hand, love sudden warm spells when the roads turn to glare ice and everybody runs into everybody else.

During cold spells I usually hunker down at home with a good supply of food and books. I don't try to run my car. If I need to go downtown I just bundle up and walk the few blocks. It's rather fun.

My car was winterized and so was my furnace. Andrew came over evenings the week before Thanksgiving to help with baking. He made ice cream for the pumpkin pie, using my unheated garage as a walk-in freezer. We've had happier Thanksgivings. I'm sure we were all thinking of the new participant we would have next year: an eleven-month-old infant in a highchair. I was looking forward to the change; Andrew clearly was not. I missed his usual grinning satisfaction as he tucked into great bowls and platters of his favorite foods. Nevertheless, however glumly, he ate his share. And most of what he didn't eat I packed and sent home with him. None of us would need to cook for a week. All right by me. I had plans for that week. I had plans for the next day. Only the next day the temperature dropped to fifty degrees below zero. And the next day, and the next.

During periods of deep cold, much of our lives goes into a kind of suspension. Every morning long lists of cancelled meetings are announced over the radio. Then there is the joy of ice fog. Ice fog is composed of all the frozen particulates from automobile exhausts and chimney smoke and all the moisture in the air. In other words, frozen smog. Don't get the idea that it's a solid wall of ice, but it might as well be; it's almost impenetrable.

Imagine trying to go to the grocery store. First, if your garage is not heated, you plug in the circulating heater of your car for an hour or two. Then, if you're lucky, and have a good car, it starts, very reluctantly, after the second or third try, just as you are about to give up. You try to back it out of the garage, and it stalls.

Eventually you get it running and you back it out and leave it to warm up, hoping it will slow down to an idle and not catch fire, as some cars have been known to do, and that nobody steals it. You let it idle for about ten minutes, adding to the ice fog. You are now ready to set out on your adventure.

All bundled up in down parka, insulated boots, mittens, and scarf, you mount the driver's seat. The inside of the car is no warmer than the outside air. You give it gas and try to move forward, but the tires are flat on the bottom. You don't let that stop you; you just keep on going, klop, klop, klop. Eventually the tires warm up enough to regain their proper shape, and the noise stops. Time now to think about the ice fog.

As you back out of the driveway you look right and left, and right again, but see nothing, not even the street lights. You start a slow crawl out into the street, but a car looms out of nowhere. You don't see it until it's four feet away. Eventually you inch your way out and nobody clobbers you, so you keep going. Or somebody clobbers you, and you don't. Let's assume you make it.

You get out to Airport Way, and you can't tell whether the light is red or green. You follow the car in front, hoping he knows what he is doing. You stay with the traffic flow, hardly getting out of first gear. Some damn fool passes you at high speed. You see him farther down the road; he has hit someone, and the police add to the hazard by scaring the hell out of you with their flashing lights, which you don't see until you are almost on top of them.

Your windshield begins to frost up on the inside. You steer with one hand and scrape with the other. You try not to breathe: that makes it worse. You can't see the edge of the road and nearly side-swipe a car that has stalled. It has no lights on. You couldn't see them if they were. You pass another stalled car, and another. Then you start to notice snakes on the snow in front of your headlights. Broken fan belts. It's not unusual for auto parts shops to run out of this commodity if a cold snap lasts too long.

All of this is just to explain why I decided to stay home. Indefinitely. It's not that I am more cowardly than the next person, I just don't go looking for trouble.

For the entire next week the temperature was fifty degrees below zero. And the next. The ice fog thickened. Planes stopped landing at the airport and fewer trucks braved the Alaska Highway. Grocery stores ran out of fresh milk and fruit and vegetables. Mail was late coming and going. The schools didn't close, as they would have down in the Lower 48, but attendance was optional; it averaged about twenty-five percent. Plumbers and furnace repairmen got rich working around the clock, thawing frozen pipes and starting recalcitrant furnaces. There wasn't a new fan belt left in town.

The cold spell lasted eighteen days. The mayor tried to have us declared a disaster area but on the whole didn't get too much sympathy. Newspapers, local and stateside, and national television ran stories about our outdoor hot tub parties—the preferred hot tubs being on hillside decks high above the city. The guests, waist deep in hot water, heads engulfed in clouds of steam, toasted the frigid minus fifty-five and colder temperatures with champagne. I don't imagine that aided the mayor's efforts.

Eventually the temperature warmed up to a springlike minus thirty, and people emerged from their dens as if from hibernation. As a matter of fact, I could give you the names of a few people who slept through the whole thing. One old sourdough who hated to chop wood kept his cabin barely above freezing and spent the entire cold spell in bed reading. He said he read with one hand under the blankets and the other holding the book. When the book hand got cold, he'd switch hands.

I spent hours working on my book; I organized and reorganized, I wrote and rewrote, but every time I approached my hypothetical murderer I took such a fright I wanted to hide under the bed. More and more I felt that even as I followed in his tracks, he was following in mine.

Anyway, time now to get on with the show. The white paint had disappeared out of my hair. I would visit Marian Aldrich and Marcia Wayman, in that order, and *then* I was going to visit the university, the scene of the crime. Crimes. Accidents. Oh, you know what I mean.

Chapter 20

*"I fled him down the labyrinthine ways," I said to my good
old friend, the suave and never-failing gear shift.*

Before I could get my act together the temperature dropped to
fifty below zero again, but I didn't care. I'd waited long enough,
and besides, I needed some groceries. I made a list and then dressed
warmly: long johns, wool slacks, socks, sweater, down parka, insulated boots and mittens, scarf, hat. I put the grocery list in my purse,
then decided I might as well go to the bank, too. I picked up the coins
I had rolled, some time before, and dropped them in my purse. Then
I added a flashlight, just for good measure. Rosy-fingered dawn was
just making her appearance as I left the house at ten-thirty.

Marian Aldrich is another of the Oysters who must be in her
midsixties. Rumor has it that she is somewhat older than Doctor,
and although he spends a lot of time and money in his attempts
to maintain a youthful appearance, he always looks as if he's just
emerged from the ministrations of a talented undertaker. Marian
doesn't help her own case much, either, the way she dresses. She
doesn't care what she wears, as long as it's recycled. I mean, the older
the better. Definitely vintage. It gives her a certain maidenly look.
She could step right into a Tennessee Williams play.

Basically, Marian and Doctor live separate lives in separate houses: he has one wing, she has the other. He spends most of his time
at their Birch Lake cabin, a big fancy place to which Marian is never
invited. They never go anywhere together; she appears to be little

more than his housekeeper. Of course she has a certain status as the wife of a physician, and she clearly enjoys it.

Marian was glad to see me. Doctor was in Hawaii at a medical convention, and Marian had been alone all through the cold spell. I could see that she was tired. And lonely. I suppose Doctor is better than no one, but she ought to get a dog. She had just made a batch of blueberry muffins.

"I must have known you were coming." She smiled. We had a nice visit over coffee and muffins and discussed everything under the sun except writing. I was trying to get a bead on anything about Marian that would make her a good suspect, but no luck. She was so prim, so docile, I can't imagine anything arousing her to a murderous pitch. I guess the woman who can live with Doctor can stand anything. She doesn't seem to realize that her marriage is different. She's even critical of people who get divorced.

"I don't think there's any problem a married couple can't work out by talking it over," she said once, to the Oysters at large. "Thank God Doctor and I have always been able to talk." I bet that's all they've been able to do. I have a theory that a lot more couples would stay together, like Marian and Doctor, if they lived in separate wings, or in duplexes, with a buffer zone between, meeting only for an occasional meal and budget conference.

Marian finally got around to the subject of my book, as I knew she would. She asked me if I was going to stick with the mystery. I gave her a resounding "Yes!"

"A lot of people could be offended if you write about friends and local people. You might not even have any friends left. Is it worth it?"

"Marian, who will ever know what I write? No one but the Oysters ever sees my work. Are they going to spread it all over town that Heather Adams made disparaging comments about various Fairbanksans in her unpublished manuscript? And anyway, do you think for one minute that there is going to be a single unkind word about anyone in my book? You know I'm not that kind of person."

She didn't seem entirely convinced, about me or the book, but we dropped the subject, and when I left soon afterwards we were still friends. But as I drove away I tallied up: Joan, the Williams sisters, Florence, Abbie, and now Marian, all hinted broadly that I should give up the mystery.

Some months ago I might have listened, but now they'd made me angry. I couldn't help thinking about one of my favorite Greeks, Hippokleides. At the feast celebrating his engagement to Kleisthenes' daughter, he drank a little too much wine and danced on his head on a table. When Kleisthenes saw the feet of his son-in-law elect waving in the air, he took umbrage.

"O son of Tisandros, you have danced away your marriage!" he shouted. The famous reply, "Hippokleides doesn't care!" expressed my feelings perfectly; I no longer gave a damn what they thought. I didn't go so far as to say I would write the book even if it killed me. I remembered what happened the last time I said that.

I definitely had a chip on my shoulder as I drove toward Marcia Wayman's house, which is located on a wooded lot off Yankovich Road, behind the university. Her pickup was parked in the driveway, but it looked as if it hadn't been moved in several days. Probably she hadn't been driving it during the cold spell.

I walked up the long drive—I avoid trouble by staying out of places where I might get stuck—and banged on her door several times, but there was no response. I turned to leave and was halfway down the drive when a huge husky came charging from behind the cabin, barking and snarling viciously. I took to my heels and got to the car before he did, but not into the car. There wasn't time. I stepped on the bumper and climbed up onto the hood but the frenzied creature still managed to sink his teeth into my leg. I yanked free, leaving shredded pants and some leg in his mouth. Crazy with fright and pain, I slipped my bag off my shoulder and swung it, hard. It caught him at the top of a great leap into the air. His head turned completely around and he fell like a bucket of lead and just lay there.

The blood poured from the back of my leg as I stood watching. He didn't move. I climbed down, took off my scarf, and tied it tightly around my leg. Then I clumsily and painfully got back in the car and drove slowly to Dr. Francis Pine's clinic.

Countless stitches, one tetanus shot, and one penicillin shot later, he and I debated whether I needed rabies shots. I won. So I was spared for the time being the rabies shot—you know where they go, everyone knows—which would have been the crowning indignity. His office notified the police, who said they would try to pick up the dog.

The whole episode had been a horrible experience, one of the most terrifying of my life. I was weak all over, my knees had the consistency of jelly, and I'm sure shock came into it too. Nevertheless, I refused to let the doctor's nurse call Rowe to come pick me up. How would he view this latest misadventure? It could be the final faggot on the fire—damned alliteration at a time like this—that was building to destroy me. And yet, what had I done wrong? Am I never to pay social calls on my friends? Does the penalty for not calling ahead have to be a murderous attack by a stray dog?

Suppose Marcia had been there; would the outcome have been any different? The whole thing had happened so fast, I'm not sure she could have prevented it.

My leg was thickly bandaged from my midcalf to my hip. I managed to get myself home, ply myself with some brandy, and even get my clothes off. My slacks were a lost cause. I reached my bed and stretched out face down. No more hot soaks for quite a while. That had to be the unkindest cut. I took one of the doctor's little pills, and knew no more.

Recuperating is getting to be a way of life with me. At least this time no one knew about it but my doctor and the canine patrol, who phoned me shortly after nine the next morning. The police had the body of the dog. When the Animal Control officers got to Marcia's they found her with the corpse, about to build a funeral pyre in her back yard. She said that when she returned home the night before she had found that her dog had escaped his tether. She called him, and when he didn't come, went looking for him. She found his frozen corpse in her driveway. He appeared to have a broken neck and/or a fractured skull. Someone had entered her yard and murdered her dog. Who was it? When the police told her, she was very angry. She finally allowed them to remove the corpse. Tests would determine if he'd had rabies.

I switched off the phone and resolved not to answer the door, at least not until I felt strong enough to face Marcia. No doubt I would be hearing from her, soon. And Rowe, too. Rowe had a key, but I hoped he wouldn't use it for a while.

I had a groggy day. The pain was so great I had to take several of the little pills. One or twice I thought I heard someone pounding on the door. Each time I lay shaking in my bed until the caller went away. Then I dozed some more. Late in the evening I heard someone fiddling with the door latch, but it was only Rowe using his key. He scolded me for forgetting to switch on the phone, but since he couldn't see the bandaged leg under the bedclothes, there were no recriminations. He switched on the phone, and it rang right while he was sitting there. I had to answer it, and naturally, it was Marcia.

What a tirade. She said her valuable guard dog was dead because I was making unannounced calls on the Oysters, all because of my stupid book, and if I had dropped the project when the Oysters told me to, this wouldn't have happened. I had no business being in her yard, and she held me completely responsible for the death of her dog.

She spoke so loudly I had to hold the phone away from my ear. I'm sure Rowe heard some of it.

"Sounds like you have at least one enemy, Mother. Better watch your step!" Satisfied that I was all right, he took his leave. Then, out of all the gloom, a thought struck me. Marcia was the first Oyster to show real anger. Of course, I had to kill her dog to find out, but I now had my prime suspect, and maybe even my killer. On that happy thought I rolled over and went to sleep.

I guess Marcia spread the story. I got several calls from the Oysters. Joan Van Blarcom said, "I did warn you, Heather." No she didn't. Not in so many words. No one warned me of physical danger if I kept on with the book. And this whole thing with the dog was a fluke. Who could have foreseen that?

I lay around for four days, then it was time to go back for a return bout with Dr. Pine. I got dressed—my writing was certainly taking a toll of my slacks, as well as my body—and picked up my purse. It jingled noisily. No wonder: it was full of loose coins. I had hit that unfortunate creature with eight rolls of quarters and a flashlight.

Chapter 21

*Is it possible, I wondered ... that after being tricked, lied to, fouled,
and muted upon, the human mind might be ready to reassert itself?*

I made the run to the clinic, where I got a new set of bandages and
another shot of antibiotic. Home again, there was nothing I felt
like doing, so I stretched out on my bed, face down, and fell asleep.
When I woke I knew exactly what I would do next. First, I would
resign from the Oysters. My wounded spirit couldn't take any more
abuse; neither could my wounded body.

Second, I would go to the University of Alaska campus, where I
would visit the places frequented by the three victims and also check
out the incidence of tall blond male students. Then I would go to the
registrar's office and try to get copies of the boys' records. I wasn't
eager for an encounter with Joan Van Blarcom, but if I had to do it,
well, so be it. And if I felt particularly brave, I would call on Philip
Van Blarcom. He might remember the three boys, and who knows,
he might have something of value to tell me.

There would most likely be an unpleasant confrontation with
Marcia Wayman, too. She was the secretary to the biology department. But all this was days away. Parking was difficult on campus,
and I was in no shape to negotiate seventy-two steps up the hill from
the lower parking lot, or the hill up to the dorms, or even the distance between buildings. But at least I knew what I was going to do.
I just didn't know when.

I sensed somehow that I was nearing the end of the trail. I was going back to where everything had started: the dormitories where the boys had lived, the dining hall where they taken their meals, the library where they had studied, their classrooms, the gym where they had engaged in their varied sports, and the paths they had crisscrossed, walking to and from their activities. Would I feel their presence? I wondered. Looking into those three pairs of blue eyes in the police station, almost eight months ago, had started me on this long and arduous quest. Perhaps I would find the end of it on the University of Alaska campus. I had to try.

❈ ❈ ❈ ❈ ❈ ❈

A week later I was better able to navigate, but the stitches still felt tight and I hurt every time I stretched, or sat, or stood up, or bent over. The temperature held steady at minus fifty and seemed determined never to rise again. I stayed home until I could stand it no longer. Finally, I decided that with my new car, if I avoided the rush hours and dressed very carefully, I could safely pull it off: I would go to the university in the morning. And while the resolve was still on me, I sat down and wrote a note to the Oysters, telling them that from now on they weren't going to have Heather Adams to kick around anymore. I left the note in plain view, so I'd remember to mail it in the morning.

Chapter 22

The smartest of all hide-and-seek artists is Death. We don't even hear his call, "Ready or not, here I come."

I set the timer and plugged in the car before I went to bed. And I set my alarm clock. I rarely oversleep, but—sometimes—I think I don't know myself anymore. I woke up right on schedule, had some coffee and a bowl of oatmeal, and put on my best cold-weather survival outfit, including down-filled long johns and two pairs of wool socks. Wool slacks, of course. I will have to replenish my supply one of these days, if I live long enough.

The temperature held at minus fifty degrees and the ice fog was thick as the proverbial pea soup. So said the radio and so said my eyes and nose. Older people, small children, people with asthma, bronchitis, and other lung problems all were warned to stay indoors. However, there was a predicted warming trend, and by midafternoon the temperature could rise to minus thirty, with some lessening of the ice fog. Good. But I wouldn't wait. Sometimes the weather people don't deliver.

The car, being new, started after one grudging chug. I backed it out of the garage and let it warm up for ten minutes or so, then I started out. I managed to back into the street without getting clobbered, and I made it over to Airport Way safely, although I could barely see the headlights of oncoming cars. In the lighter traffic of 10:30 a.m., and with half of Fairbanks staying home because of the temperature, the four-mile drive to the university still took forty minutes, but I made it, which was more than I could say for all the cars stalled by the side of the road. And I did have to park in the lower parking lot, and I did have to climb those killer steps, all seventy-two of them.

I went into the Great Hall in the Fine Arts Complex, which is right across the street from the top of those cursed steps, and sat down for a few minutes to catch my breath. The Fine Arts Complex is composed of the Great Hall, theater, concert hall, music and art departments, and the public radio and television stations. A long hallway connects with the library.

I didn't see any tall blond men as I sat there, because everyone who came through the doors was engulfed in a foggy cloud and muffled in thick parkas with hoods drawn forward. Many had scarves tied over their mouths and noses; a few wore ski masks. So much for that idea.

I was tired, but I forced myself to walk the long hall to the library, then outside and across the campus to the Bunnell Building, where Joan Van Blarcom held sway in the registrar's office. At precisely 11:30 I asked the young secretary for the records of Mark Sandberg, Jason Calloway, and William Hodgson. I explained who they were and why I needed their files. She said she would have to discuss it with Mrs. Van Blarcom, who had just left for a luncheon meeting and would not be back before one-thirty or even later.

With all that time to spare, I decided to walk up the hill to Bartlett and Moore Halls, where two of the boys had lived. I soon repented of that decision. While ice fog isn't a problem up here on the campus hill, getting up that hill was. I had to move slowly; age, bulky clothing, and sore spots all worked against me. Bent almost double, my glasses all frosted up, and the scarf over my mouth and nose wringing wet, I was passed by a stream of ghostly figures, striding long youthful strides. I felt like grabbing hold of a passing coattail and hitching a ride.

The cold began to penetrate my layers of insulation. My fingertips felt cold first, then my feet. Painful. Numbing. I was almost crawling on all fours by the time I made it up the steps of Bartlett Hall. Once inside, I dropped down on a couch and promptly fell asleep. Or was it a trance? Those old images returned, of three boys standing side by side on the stone battlements in front of the building, laughingly throwing barrages of snowballs down on their adversaries below. I sprawled there, I don't know how long, watching the phantoms of three boys I had come to know, to care about, and to mourn. In my last sighting of the three they had their arms around each other's shoulders, as I had first seen them; three pairs of the bluest eyes, staring into mine. I knew what they wanted. I would do my best. They disappeared, and I awoke. A half hour had passed.

I walked over to the entrance and looked out through the glass doors, but nobody was there, no blond blue-eyed boys, only a few students walking up the concrete steps. Muffled students were coming and going all around me. No one noticed the tired old lady, but no one acted as if I didn't belong there, either. I decided to complete the project by walking next door to Moore Hall. The two buildings were connected; the same concrete steps and outer court served both. That entrance hall too was full of students coming and going, milling around. I sat down in a wooden chair that wasn't piled with books, for a few minutes, with my eyes closed, and had more visions of blond boys, huddled over books, watching television, entering and leaving the elevator, carrying bags of laundry.

I realized then that maybe people were right about me: maybe I was cracking up. I had visions of dead people, I was paranoid, accident prone, and maybe I *was* suicidal. Maybe I was all of those things, but suddenly I understood what my subconscious had been trying to tell me for some time: those three boys *had been murdered*. Of course they had; I was sure of it. I'd known it all along. Today I'd take a step in the right direction: I would call on Philip Van Blarcom, although I couldn't exactly say where he fitted into the scheme of things. Nor could I see how the Oysters were involved, but some of them had to be.

I was getting overheated in my heavy clothing, so I left. As I descended the concrete stairs I looked over toward the parking area to see if any cars were heading out. Had there been one I would have begged a ride. But there wasn't. Every car looked as if it had been parked for days, if not weeks. I started downhill toward the main campus.

If anything, downhill was more difficult than uphill. Well, I was more tired now. My legs were weak and seemed to wobble every which way. The soaking wet scarf felt terrible. I pulled it off and breathed in the frigid air. That felt even worse. I began to get pains in my chest. I felt light-headed and a bit silly. I caught myself humming *"Nero, My Dog, Has Fleas,"* which is as close as a Unitarian heretic can come to *Nearer, My God, To Thee.* Same good tune. I stumbled the last few hundred feet to the Wood Center, where I removed my parka and collapsed in a big overstuffed chair. Hours later (my watch said twenty past one), I put my parka back on and returned to the Bunnell Building and Joan Van Blarcom.

I wasn't eager to see her. I remembered her "I did warn you, Heather," about the dog incident, and here I was, hard at it again. And how did I know she wasn't the murderer? In for a penny, in for a pound. She wasn't back yet.

"Come back in half an hour," the girl said, frostily. I liked that *frostily*. So apt.

At least I was warmed up. What could I do in a half-hour? I could go to the library, where I could just sit and absorb the ambience. I could see if there were any tall blond students. Or any tall blond ghosts.

I left Bunnell and walked across the campus. passing snow-covered mounds which, when sumer is y-cumin in, sport riots of flowers. And giant cabbages. With nests of robins in their hair. Safely in the warm library, I settled down on a comfortable couch in the magazine section. I meditated. I dozed. I meditated some more. I dozed some more.

The half-hour had become an hour. The short walk back to Bunnell seemed longer this time. I couldn't believe Joan when I saw her. She'd looked bad enough when I'd called on her several weeks ago; now she looked like a ghost, too. All I ever seemed to see anymore were ghosts. She couldn't believe me, either.

"My god, Heather, what are you doing out in this cold? You look terrible! Here, sit down. You need some hot coffee." She pushed me into a chair. A secretary held a hot cup to my lips.

"I've come to get the files of the three students who were—"

"Heather, you must be mad! Fifty below zero, and that's all you have to think about! I can't let you have them."

"Fine. Who is your boss? I'll ask him."

She sat there looking at me as if I were some prehistoric lizard. I suppose that's what I looked like. Felt like it, too. I don't know where I got the nerve, or the energy. I out-stared her.

"I don't know where the files are. Come back on Monday."

"No. Monday may be just as cold as today, if not colder. What do you want to do, kill me?" She looked at me as if she wasn't sure of the answer, but I won again.

"Come back in an hour, then. I'll see what I can do. It won't be easy." I felt terribly weak and lightheaded. Nevertheless I decided to warm up the car. If I left it too long in this cold I wouldn't be able to start it. I made my way out to that stairway to hell. I stood at the top, looking down those ten thousand fucking steps. I wondered if I should fly, or better yet, jump. Better not. Probably against the rules. Hang on to the railing. Plant each foot ve - ry carefully. Stop breathing: it hurts too much. Maybe a little song will help. *Nero, my dog has fleas. Nero has fleas. Darkness be over me, My rest a stone.*

So hard to unlock the car. So hard to climb in. So stiff and sore and cold. Turn the key, Heather, there's a good girl. It started. Good car. Nice car. I sat there listening to the timbre of the engine, as it stumbled over its first staccato beats, picked up, raced for a bit, and then finally settled down to a nice steady purr. *Very* good car. The cold, even in the car, was numbing. I would never make it up those steps again. Never. Then to the Great Hall, and then down that long passage to the library, and then outside and kitty-cornered across the square where the statue of Silent the Willy … Silly the … or was he at my alma mater? Then all the way over to the registrar's office. Never make it. Better just sit here and rest. Perchance to … something or other. Freeze to death. Like Jason. And Bill.

What did I care about campus rules? I would move my car over behind the Bunnell Building. If security took my car, they could have it, and me too. I'll sing a song to that.

Still all my song shall be, Nero my dog has fleas, Nero my dog has fleas, Nero has fleas.

The windshield was frosted over. I didn't care. I drove the car slowly toward the exit. After I bounced off the guard rail a time or two I opened the window and stuck my head out, warbling loudly as the hard tires klop klop klopped out of the parking lot, and up the steep, steep, winding drive to the campus. Suppose the engine stalled on the hill. What-the-hell what-the-hell what-the-hell. I would have a slippery slide all the way down. Backwards. *Toujours gai! But Old Man River, He jus' kep' rollin' along.*

"When the roll is called up yonder," I warbled, and "The Old Rugged Cross," and I concluded with "Bringing in the Sheaves" as I backed into the vice-chancellor's spot, right beside the lower door. No doubt about it, God has all the best tunes. And parking spaces.

I locked the car and entered the building. Soaking wet under my heavy clothing, I felt cold and clammy. The registrar's office was up a delightful flight of stairs. I half expected Joan to have taken a powder. She knew I would not be stopped on this issue. We will not be moved. I will not be moved, either. Or is it *shall*?

My old friend was waiting for me. She picked up the three files and met me at the counter.

"My God, you've frosted your nose. It's all white." She pushed me into a chair and clapped her hand over the offending part. She signaled the young secretary to bring coffee.

"Milk, please, and no chloral hydrate. "

"What?" She abandoned my nose and stepped back. "You took it yourself. You know you did." She was furious. Another angry Oyster.

"I'm sorry. I meant, no sugar." She put her hand back on my nose.

"All this for nothing. We can't let these files leave the office."

"That's all right," I mumbled into her hand. "Copies will do."

"I'm very busy just now. I'll have them mailed to you."

"I'll make the copies. I'm in no hurry." I looked her in the eye. Eyes. She looked at me as if undecided whether to kill me. Again.

"What's wrong with you? You should be home in bed. Or in the hospital, not out on crazy errands."

"So maybe I'm crazy. I want those files."

"Heather, we've been friends for too long to let something like … this …" she held up the files, "come between us." Then her face changed; she reached some decision.

"Let's have dinner together at the Pump House. I'll meet you at four-thirty. That's not too long from now, and I'll bring the copies of the files with me. I promise."

This was a new tack. Could I trust her? Well, why not? I agreed to meet her.

"My car is right next to the rear entrance," I said. "In the vice-chancellor's spot. I'll have it warmed up." She smiled for the first time.

"You go somewhere and sit down."

"I will. Biology Department, and Philip." Her smile froze. Big mouth. What did you tell her for? Ah well, not my best day.

The biology office was not far. Down the hall, then down the stairs. My feet were like lead. But Emily Dickinson, I mean Marcia Wayman, was at her desk, right where she belonged. I walked over to her and drew myself up to my full six-foot-two. Five-foot-two. I looked her square in the eye. Eyes. A few times in my life I have demonstrated vestigial signs of courage, and that was one of them. But I think I was slightly mad by then.

"Marcia," I said, weakly, "I want to explain, to apologize." Well, she wasn't about to make a scene there in the office. She shoved a chair under me before I could fall.

"Sit down, Heather. I'm just about to have a cup of coffee. How about you?" I nodded with relief. She didn't ask me if I wanted chloral hydrate, and I didn't volunteer. She came back a couple of minutes later with two steaming mugs, and handed one to me. She loosened my parka and untied my scarf.

"My god, Heather, you ought to be home in bed. Listen to your breathing."

"I'm listening. Marcia, your dog … it was a … horrible accident. Never killed … anything … in my life … except a few fish…." And I began to cry over that damned murdering dog. I tried to explain what had happened that terrible afternoon, but I don't think I was very intelligible. She listened intently, but interrupted before I finished.

"Heather, if you hadn't been snooping around for that book of yours—and we did ask you to stop—it never would have happened."

"It could have happened—to someone else."

"Austen knew everyone who came to the house. He had never attacked anyone before. He would only attack if someone threatened me."

"I didn't—I wasn't—" I leaned back and took a deep, painful breath. "I'd just stopped in for a little visit."

"Why, Heather?" I didn't answer.

Several students stopped by Marcia's desk to pick up some sort of assignments. She gave them directions, and they took off. She turned back to me.

"I wanted to ask if you … remembered … ever … meeting any of … the three boys."

"Hardly. Those boys were freshmen, and it takes a while to get all the new students sorted out. They weren't here long enough."

"Marcia, those boys were … murdered. I think the third boy, William, fell into a snow dump, like the one … on Wendell Street. That's where his body was … all that time. I'm sure of it. Do you know why … he … would have been climbing … on a snow dump?"

"How would I know? Maybe he was looking for ice worms."

"Yes. Well. Thank you, Marcia." I took a big swallow of coffee and nearly choked. "Please ask Philip Van Blarcom if he will see me. I have … a few questions … for him."

I wish I could describe the look on her face. Fury? Impatience? Whatever it was, she sat there drumming her fingers on the desk, and looking me full in the face. Then she seemed to make up her mind about something. She stood up and walked down the hall, I suppose to his office. Seconds later she returned.

"He's not here, but he could be back any time. If you'll wait, I think we can get you in for a few minutes."

Fine. I sure didn't mind a little more rest. Or warmth. I picked up a college catalog and thumbed through it. I must have dozed off again. The sound of the catalog hitting the floor woke me.

Four o'clock. I still had a half-hour before going to meet Joan. Marcia, meanwhile, seemed not to have noticed my little nap. She was even friendly. She said she understood about the dog. If only he hadn't gotten loose. I offered to buy her a new one.

"Thanks, Heather, but loving things, and people, just complicates life." More for Marcia than for most people, I thought. I had a sudden impulse.

"Marcia," I asked, "Do you have any idea why the Van Blarcoms separated?" I waited for the explosion. It came.

"Heather, if I had any idea, which I don't, of what happened between the Van Blarcoms, I certainly wouldn't tell you, or anyone else."

I got up to leave.

"Don't go, Heather. It's just that I take my work very seriously. I would never pry into his … their … business. I'll see if he's here." She walked back to Philip Van Blarcom's office. She returned smiling.

"He's back. He'll be out to get you in a minute, as soon as he finishes a long-distance phone call. If you'll excuse me, I have to leave early. I have an appointment." She walked over to a coat closet and pulled out a down parka and some boots.

"Do you have your pickup, Marcia?"

"No, I just walk. It's easier than fighting a car. Isn't it?" She had a point. She quickly donned several layers of clothing and topped them off with the parka, scarf, and mittens.

"Toss me your keys. I'll start your car for you. Where did you park it?" I told her, and handed over the keys.

"Don't forget to lock it," I reminded her. "I have another set of keys in my bag." And with a cheery wave, she was gone. A good day's work, I thought. Dinner with Joan, practically reconciled with Marcia, I'd soon have the files, and best of all, an interview with Philip Van Blarcom. I settled down to wait.

I busied myself again with the catalog. There were a lot of pictures of students, but none I recognized. There were many different courses of study. I think I found the one the three boys were following, if they were science majors, as I assumed they were. I looked at my watch: four twenty-five. I stood up and walked back to Philip Van Blarcom's office. He wasn't there. He must have forgotten all about me. Damn. Nothing to do but give up on him for now and go meet

Joan. I zipped up my parka, picked up my mittens and scarf, and left by the lower door where my car was parked.

The car was still running. A rush of warm air hit me as I opened the door, which Marcia had forgotten to lock. Well, no harm done. As I waited for Joan, I looked out over the brow of the hill, at one of the most beautiful sights in the world, the city lights of Fairbanks. Suddenly those lights went out.

※ ※ ※ ※ ※ ※

I opened one eye, quietly. And then the other. I was in the idiot's seat of a Cessna 180, and Joan Underwood was the pilot. She grasped the stick so intently she didn't see me open my eyes. The engine noise drowned out the sound of my thinking. We weren't going to dinner, after all. Just as well. I couldn't eat a thing. Wherever she was taking me, I wasn't coming back. I had hoped to see my new grandchild, but no matter. I was so tired. I closed my eyes for the last time.

Chapter 23

The members all wear buttons with the initials
CAIC. ... It means, Christ am I confused.

I had a splitting headache. There was a strange noise in my head, like a trio of chainsaws. I was nauseous. Someone held a pan to my mouth just in time to catch the eruption. She said something to me but I ignored her and turned away. She left.

"Good morning, Heather." I turned to see who it was. Dennis Wheeler was sitting beside my bed. I turned away again. What was he doing in heaven? Besides, I didn't believe in heaven.

"You're in the hospital." I didn't care where I was.

"You were brought in last night, in pretty bad shape."

So? Who cares? Not I.

"It was touch and go for a while. You're going to be okay now. You really got it this time. Want to hear about it?"

"This time?"

"Good lord, woman, in the years I've lived next door to you, you've never had a single accident, not counting that business with the canoe."

"You said I ... got it ... this time?"

Visions of that last flight came flooding back. I remembered who was piloting the plane, and tears came into my eyes.

"Maybe you're not ready for this." He stood up.

"Wait."

He sat down, "Since you insist."

"Why?"

"My god, Heather, you were about to expose a triple murderer, that's why."

"You said I ... got it ... this time?"

"That's what I said. In the last three months you've had three accidents. Any one of them could have been fatal. They weren't accidents. They were intended to finish you off."

This brought another flood of tears. I couldn't help it. He handed me a wad of tissues. I wiped my eyes.

"I knew they were murdered. They had to have been. But the Oysters ..."

"Knew all about it. Some of them. One of them, at least. A couple more. You had it all laid out, right down to the last T. After we got you settled in the hospital last night, I went over to your house to see if I could find your notes. Guess what! Someone else was already there. We had a bit of a tussle, and she's now in jail, charged with breaking and entering, assault with intent to kill, and I don't think we'll have any trouble making a murder charge stick." He waited for some comment from me, but I had none. He continued.

"After I finished at the jail I went back to your house, and I found the notes for your mystery. I read them, and also the first six chapters. Now, don't get me wrong, Heather. Your mystery is a great book, what there is of it, but the notes are something else. You had every detail of those killings down in black and white."

Was this supposed to make me feel good? I felt worse every second.

"I spent the whole night studying your papers. It took me an hour to figure out that honest mare of Pharsalus ..."

He looked at me in awe.

"Aristotle had it wrong, didn't he? The mare turned out to be a stallion. Well, the Aristotle did it. Who else but Professor Van Blarcom? Tall, blond, athletic, scientific? So I phoned him, even though it was six in the morning, and he said to come on over. And I got the whole story, the parts you couldn't get."

He stopped. I suppose he wanted me to beg him for the rest, but I didn't want to hear it. I turned to the wall and tears began to flow again.

"Van Blarcom told me all about his marriage to Joan, Mrs. Van Blarcom, that is, how happy they were, twenty years ago. Whatever it was. A perfect marriage, he said. I guess she was some knockout. They must have been a good-looking pair, both tall and blond, slim, athletic, and all. They were very popular, had a busy social life. They built a big house near the campus, they had a whole lot of pets—Joan, Mrs. Van Blarcom, loved animals. They had everything, except kids. A perfect marriage. Then when they were married one, two years, his wife, Mrs. Van Blarcom, started drinking. Just out of the blue." He paused to see if I was taking it all in.

"One night the professor came home from a meeting and found his wife drunk and every animal in the house dead. The little kitten had its neck broken. Same with a pair of lovebirds, their necks wrung, both of them. In their cage. Out in the yard their big husky was dead too, tied in front of his kennel. His head bashed in. The wooden club was right there. Well, when she sobered up, Joan, Mrs. Van Blarcom, denied killing her pets and carried on something awful, but he knew." He paused again, but I didn't respond. He went on anyway.

"Well, she went on the wagon for several months, and begged for another dog—she really liked animals when she was herself—and against his better judgment, he gave in. Some months later, he came home from a meeting, and there was Joan, drunk, and the dog dead, outside by his kennel. Just like before. Clubbed. She denied it again, of course, but she did agree to get treatment for her drinking, and it worked, and she never had any more trouble. Lots of people don't even know about it. But the professor, with his interest in genetics, well, he figured her for some kind of manic-depressive type, not a good candidate for motherhood. She might pass on her tendency to their children. But instead of laying the blame on her, because he didn't want to hurt her feelings, he told her there was this hereditary disease in *his* family. Lou Gehrig's disease. His father and brother both died of it, he said, and as that happened before they were married, he hadn't told her, because he was afraid she might have decided not to marry him. He told her they really shouldn't have any children." He paused. "He figured that was the kindest way to go about it."

"Well, it was a real blow to her, especially since she had designed that big house to be filled up with kids and animals. But she accepted his decision and never mentioned children again. He said she was always more quiet after that, and changed, somehow. I guess you noticed it too." I nodded.

"Not long after that the professor got a phone call from this medical doctor friend of his. He was treating this couple, a captain and his wife on Eielson Air Force Base, for infertility." He paused.

"The couple were both tall and blond, and that's what made him think of the professor. Well, the doctor talked the professor into being a sperm donor. Naturally, the professor didn't tell his wife, because he'd lied to her about his not wanting kids, and he figured that being military, the couple would be leaving the area anyway. I have a sneaking suspicion the professor considered himself a good candidate ... ah ... genetically speaking, unlike his wife, Mrs. Van Blarcom. Altogether, over the next year and a half, he figured he was a sperm donor about four or five times. Then the medical doctor moved out of Alaska, and that was that."

I could see where all this was leading, and I didn't want to hear it. But he wouldn't shut up.

"The professor actually forgot about all the sperm donor business, and life went on as usual. Which wasn't all that great. Then three years ago, Joan, Mrs. Van Blarcom, came home from work—she's the registrar at the University—oh, sure, you know all about that—and told the professor that this kid had showed up, a freshman, who was the spitting image of the professor when he was young. She said the kid could pass for his son. The professor said he doesn't know what came over him, why he decided to tell the truth after all those years, but anyway, he told her. About lying to her, about being a sperm donor, and all. That the kid could be his son. Probably was. He was the right age. You following this?"

I was crying so hard I could hardly hear him, but I nodded.

"Well, the professor said something broke in her. He saw it happen. She never said a word of reproach. She just quietly packed up and moved out. A few weeks later the boy was found dead. Suicide." I blew my nose. Would he never stop?

"And he figured it *was* suicide. He didn't know any better. But when the second boy enrolled in one of the professor's classes a year later, the professor recognized him right away. He looked up the boy's records, and sure enough, he was born on Eielson, eighteen years before. All his chickens were coming home to roost, so to speak." I blotted my face.

"When this boy died too, the professor was sure it was murder, even though it looked like an accident, and after the third one, he was positive. He had no proof, but he was pretty sure it was his wife, Mrs. Van Blarcom. But you, I can't believe the way you had it all figured out."

The nurse came in then and, finding me in tears, chased Dennis out. She insisted I take a pill. Then she plumped up my pillow, turned out the light and left, closing the door behind her. I lay there, I don't know how long, in some kind of dream world where none of this had ever happened.

Chapter 24

Is it possible, I wondered ... that after being tricked, lied to, fouled and muted upon, the human mind might be ready to reassert itself?

Eventually, I suppose I dozed off. I don't know for how long, but when I awoke I felt a little better. Not good, just not as bad. I would never feel good again. I was lying there inwardly blaming myself for everything when the door to my room opened. A ghostly figure, all hooded and robed, quietly entered and walked silently to my bedside. It stood there looking down at me. I had trouble seeing in the dark, and I couldn't seem to focus my eyes.

"Who are you?" I croaked. But I knew who it was. And I knew what she wanted. It was the ghost of Joan Van Blarcom. Why didn't Dennis tell me she was dead? Although why would she want to live, after all she had done?

I was so completely paralyzed I couldn't scream; I couldn't even breathe. She quietly looked me up and down, as if surveying her handiwork and finding it wanting. How little we all know each other, in the end. The ghost pushed her hood back, and loosened her robe. Then she spoke, in a whisper.

"I came to thank you for all that you have done for me."

"I never meant to do any of it. It was all accidental."

"No one would ever have known anything if you hadn't decided to write that book. I can hardly ignore what you've done; intentional or not, you've changed everything for me."

"You can't ignore the effect of your own actions."

"No. If only I had more of what you have. Courage. Guts. Things might have been different. They might still be alive."

"Would it have taken so much courage to let them live?"

I relaxed a little and let my body sink into the bedding. Why fight it? I didn't care any more.

She looked puzzled. "I'd give anything to bring them back, anything."

"But you can't."

"No. But I can square things with you."

"Is that why you're here?" She nodded.

"How did you die?"

"Heather, I'm not dead. Look at me." A delusional ghost. I gave up.

"Joan, I'm tired. Do what you came to do. I won't fight you."

I closed my eyes and sank deeper into the mattress. Once again I thought about my new grandchild. But no matter. I commended my soul to oblivion.

I felt movement, a weight on my bed. Then something wet and rough covered my nose and swished back and forth. I opened my eyes. A small husky puppy sat on my pillow, next to my face, and he was trying to lick me to death.

"That's a funny way to kill someone."

"Kill? What are you talking about, kill?"

"Dennis Wheeler said you were in jail. That you had killed the three boys and had tried to kill me."

"Heather, I don't know what you are talking about, but believe me, you're mistaken. Marcia's in jail. Apparently I've never killed anything."

I just lay there and felt a warm shock wave go up and down my body. It passed, but I was weak all over again, and soaking wet.

"He said I had everything right in my notes. I was sure the boys had been murdered, but I hadn't really decided on the murderer; I just said Marcia would be a good choice because ... but you were the one I saw flying the plane, taking me ... "

"To the hospital. I came out onto the parking lot in time to see your car drive off. I thought we must have misunderstood each other, so I got in my car and followed you. But first I had to warm it up a bit, so I fell behind. You turned toward the Pump House. When you passed the Pump House I was puzzled, but I decided to follow you anyway, or we might have lost each other completely."

"I don't remember any of this. "

"Your car finally turned off at the little park where the ice fishermen drive out on the river. I waited on the highway, expecting you to finish your errand and return; instead, after about ten minutes or so, maybe longer, a skier left the car and headed up river. I knew it wasn't you, so I waited until the skier was out of sight and then drove out onto the river. I found you sitting in the driver's seat, unconscious, with a hose running from the exhaust into the car. I detached the hose, moved you over, and headed for the hospital."

"That's why I saw you flying the plane... car..."

"Your delirium did that. You were raving."

It was a lot to assimilate, all at once.

"You saved my life."

She bowed her head.

"I still don't understand. Marcia killed the boys? I can see where you might have thought you had some reason to kill them, if you were deranged, but Marcia... what reason did she have?"

"She's been in love with Philip since long before I met him. She covered up well; I sensed it but I never let on. I knew Philip wasn't interested in her, she wasn't his type"—she sounded bitter—"and I wanted to spare her embarrassment, but even after we were married, she didn't give up. She dyed her hair blonde, she became a friend of the family and offered to watch the house, and animals, if we went anywhere. Philip used to ask her to watch me, too." She looked really angry.

"When the first boy turned up, Marcia spotted the resemblance to Philip right away. Then she saw Philip's reaction when he saw the boy the first time. I suppose he looked shocked. Embarrassed. She must have become suspicious and looked up the boy's records."

"And?"

"She thought Philip had been playing around. If he had to play around, he was supposed to play around with her. Instead he chose a couple of women on Eielson. Or so she thought. Do you remember when he used to drive down to Eielson to teach evening classes? There's no way he could have found time for any extramarital involvement; he drove down with two other men." She paused to extricate her hand from the puppy's sharp teeth.

"She may have killed the first boy to save Philip from exposure. Eventually people would have noticed his resemblance to Philip. Probably she was enraged by his very existence. What he represented. Other women could have Philip, but she couldn't."

"Joan, how could she kill...?"

"It probably wasn't too difficult. She'd killed quite a few innocent creatures by then. Then second boy showed up—"

"And the third."

"Yes. By then she was terribly sure of herself. Heather, so help me God, I thought Philip was killing his own..."

"And he thought you were killing them."

"If only we could have saved them, somehow. They should have been my sons."

She looked down at the puppy, who had gotten tired of licking my face and was chewing on her hand.

"I think she expected that eventually Philip would turn to her," she continued, "because she was always there. Always helping him. She didn't know Philip at all. Philip never loved anyone."

"Not even you?"

"Not even me. Apparently I had all the qualifications to fill the role of Dr. Philip Van Blarcom's wife. A robot could have been his wife, someone without a heart, or feelings. Just so she knew her role."

"Is that why you started drinking? "

"Philip had asked me not to fly any more and to give up my job. I had no children, I had nothing. But I recovered, eventually, and went back to work."

"When did you see Philip?"

"He came to see me this morning, after he saw that policeman, Dennis Wheeler, your neighbor. He apologized and asked me to come back."

"Are you going to?"

"No. There's been much too much ... too much has happened. I would have left him long ago if he hadn't said there was Lou Gehrig's disease in his family and that it could strike him, too. I thought I had to stay and care for him if that happened. But it was a lie."

"Joan, I'm so sorry ..."

"Don't be sorry. I'm going to get my life back at last. When I started to drink, Marcia was the only friend I had. She was very understanding. She even got me to join the Oysters. Probably so she could keep track of me."

"That's why she put out alcoholic drinks when we met at her cabin. To start you drinking again. But you never took any. No one did."

"I didn't figure that out. I never suspected her of anything, not even killing the animals. I thought I had killed them."

"How does Philip feel about all of this?"

"He's devastated, but more for himself than for anyone else. He can't believe that Marcia, his faithful dogsbody all these years ..."

"But he could believe it about you."

"Yes. But she wasn't a person to him, either. It's a pity he didn't marry her. She wouldn't have minded being 'and wife.' I asked him once why he'd married me, and he said, 'I couldn't marry just anybody.' Marcia, you see, was 'just anybody.' But what a lot of lives would have been spared."

We sat quietly for a few minutes, each thinking her own thoughts.

"He's going to leave the university and go somewhere else," she said. "He offered me the house, and I accepted."

At that, her new family jumped down from her arms and made a puddle on my bed. It spread out, wide and yellow.

"Oh, no! This is what I get for sneaking you in. I'd better get you out of here. I'm so sorry, Heather. But I had to show him to you, and thank you for—" she hesitated—"everything." She leaned over, kissed me on the cheek, and snatching up the puppy, zipped him into the front of her parka. As she slipped out the door the nurse entered and switched on the light. She looked at my bed.

"Well, really, Mrs. Adams. Couldn't you have used your buzzer?" I knew I was really alive, then. I cringe, therefore I am.

Rowe and Alice and Andrew came in after lunch. I must really have scared them this time. Alice and Rowe had come to the hospital the evening before, when I was brought in, and had stayed most of the night. They'd left when I was declared out of danger, but they still looked tired, especially Alice, who was expecting the baby in the next three weeks or so.

"Well, Ma, I hope this is the last adventure for a while. No more detecting, no more murders, no more accidents, and no more books!"

"Well, I have to finish the one I've started. After that, I'll see. I'm sorry that Alice had to go through all this stress, just now." Andrew glowered. Apparently we still did not talk about the new baby.

"By the way, Ma, some television reporters have been nosing around. You're a pretty famous character, did you know that? A real celebrity. They want you on a talk show. Good Morning…"

"America?"

"No, 'Good Morning, Fairbanks!'" We all laughed.

I still had a lot of questions, but I suddenly realized how weak I was, how totally drained.

"Do you know what I'd like to do? I'd like to go to Hawaii and soak my poor battered body in the ocean. Then I'd like to lie in the sun, and sleep, and sleep, and sleep, and then sleep some more, and …"

"And take me with you!" shouted Andrew, as he jumped on my feet. It wasn't too bad. They were the best part of me. He leaned forward and peered into my face. His elbows dug into my chest. And, God help me, I said *yes*.

Chapter 25

How much understanding and forgiveness it takes
to love anything; or vice versa, to be loved.

It was a long time before I had everything straight in my mind, because I really was sick. Not only was there the new injury to my
head and the aftermath of carbon monoxide poisoning—although,
thanks to Joan's timely interference, I hadn't gotten a really large
dose of that—I had also contracted pneumonia. And all the previous
injuries, from which I hadn't completely recovered when I went out
into the cold in pursuit of a killer, had left my normally hardy con-
stitution in less than optimal condition.

Andrew and I left for Hawaii as soon as he got out of school for
his holiday vacation, which started a few days before Christmas. I
was pushing it, but weak as I was, I preferred to recuperate in Hawaii
rather than in Fairbanks. Looking back, it was all idyllic, but when
I zero in on close-ups, I remember, among other things, his abor-
tive efforts to teach me to surfboard. I kept falling off the board and
being swept in and out by the breakers, much to the delight of a
horde of camera-bearing fellow tourists. Eventually Andrew gave
up and left me to concentrate on soaking and sunning. Then there
was the time he was escorted back to our room by hotel security; he
had commandeered an elevator and was making solo flights up and
down the fifteen floors. I considered that more or less normal behavior; his father had done the same thing.

I woke up on Christmas morning to find a Christmas tree fashioned from a branch of a tropical shrub, hung with flowers and shells and all kinds of little gleanings from the beach. I could only hope nobody's garden had been denuded. He gave me a beautiful muumuu from a nearby thrift store, and I presented him with the surfboard he'd been eyeing in the hotel gift shop.

"This means we're coming back," he said, happily.

Three weeks in Hawaii with Andrew worked miracles. The constant vigilance, the need not only to observe, but to anticipate and when possible to head off Andrew's activities did wonders for my poor brain.

Just before our return home we had a phone call from Rowe, informing us that Miss Susan Adams had arrived safely, all eight pounds of her, and mother and daughter were doing well. Andrew, I'm happy to say, didn't show any signs of comprehension until we were greeted by the lavishly festooned bassinet in their living room on our return. He refused even to look at Susan. He ran storming up the stairs to his room and hardly emerged until it was time to return to school. He survived by raiding the refrigerator at night and commiserating with his friends on the phone all day.

Returning to school helped some, but he'd promised war if the baby was a girl, and war it was. Entering the house after school, he would slam the front door and drop his books noisily on the floor, pausing just long enough to glare toward the baby, who slumbered in her bassinet across the living room. As soon as she let out a loud protest, and Andrew was satisfied that he had awakened her, he would dash up the stairs to his room.

When he finally returned to taking his meals with the family, he opened his mouth only to stuff it with food. And he never so much as glanced in the bassinet at his sister. One evening, when she was four months old, Alice bravely gave little Susan her bottle at the dinner table, and for the first time, Andrew was forced to look at her. The infant took one look at Andrew and said "Ah goo." He thought she was saying Andrew and that her very first word was his name. He may have been ready for a truce, because his sister had never even seen him before. He decided she was very intelligent, and might be a worthy candidate for some mentoring. He started checking in at her bassinet when he arrived home from school and was usually greeted by a resounding "Ahgoo!" His mother, when she discovered what was happening, displayed a new understanding of her son, and kept her distance. All her troubles were over, she thought.

Eventually Andrew's pride in his sister's accomplishments forced him to abandon attempts at secrecy and openly take credit for her precocious behavior. At five months, Susan greeted Andrew with delighted cries of "Angoo!" and she could blow her food all over her mother.

"She caught on the first time I showed her," he said, proudly. "She's really smart."

Alice began to have mixed feelings about this consummation; her pretty little daughter was as difficult to keep clean and tidy as ever Andrew had been, and she greeted admiring guests with all the funny faces and uncouth noises at her command.

One day I was sitting on their living room floor with my two grandchildren, having a great time making funny faces, trying out new sound effects, and rolling on the floor. Actually, they rolled; I just rocked a little. We were laughing hysterically with each new effort, when I heard Alice saying sadly to Rowe, in the next room, "Now there are three of them," and Rowe answered, drawing her into the living room, "Let's make it five."

Every time Dennis Wheeler stopped in for coffee, I had more questions for him, like, "What on earth prompted Marcia Wayman to risk the open attack on me that resulted in her exposure?"

"Well," answered Dennis, stroking his chin, "I think it was fear that you might get in to see Philip Van Blarcom. You had shown yourself to be very stubborn. She was sure that once you made up your mind, you'd see him, one way or another. And he might well have told you the truth about the boys. Not that she knew the truth— she thought they were the results of—ah—affairs with women. That information would have exposed Philip as the father of three out-of-wedlock sons. Even the truth, artificial insemination, which she didn't know, would have been very embarrassing for him. It could also have aroused suspicion about their deaths. And you hadn't mentioned your dinner appointment with Joan, Mrs. Van Blarcom. If she'd known that..."

"She probably wouldn't have tried it. At least I kept my mouth shut about something."

"It wouldn't have mattered except that you were really getting close."

"All that saved me was that Joan Van Blarcom saw my car driving off, and followed. But another suicide?"

"Another suicide? No one would have connected you with the suicide of that boy. That was ancient history."

"But me, a suicide?"

"Think about it, Heather. Your behavior had been, well, different, for some weeks, if not months. An automobile accident, with the suspicion that you had been drinking. An overdose of sleeping pills, whether you took them on purpose or not. That's not all. When I caught up with the lady, Miss Wayman, the murderer, in your house that night, she was reading a letter to the Oysters saying they wouldn't have Heather Adams to kick around any more. That may not sound like a suicide note to you, but it does to me."

"It was a resignation letter. I was resigning from the Oysters."

"And there right on your desk were two books all about suicide."

"I bought them to use as references for my book. Because the first student who died was an apparent suicide. It was right in my notes."

"Your notes were about to come up missing."

"The Oysters knew what was in them. They would have told."

"Don't bet on it. Marcia, Miss Wayman, had convinced your friends. She persuaded Abbie, Mrs. Buffmire, that she should boycott the book because it was causing you to have a breakdown. And Flornece, Mrs. Hokkainen—society lady, is she? She was afraid you'd involve the Oysters in some kind of a scandal. Gwladys and Gwendolyn thought that because one boy, Mark Sandberg, had worked for them, they could be charged with withholding evidence, even though Mar— Miss Wayman, was the one who talked them into withholding it. She told them it was best not to get involved in police business. That what they knew wouldn't have affected the suicide verdict."

"Mark Sandberg had worked for the Williams sisters? I knew it! Those scratches on his leg. Look!"

I held out my leg and showed him the scars Percy had engraved on my shin the day of the tea party.

"That was right in your notes, too. You didn't miss anything." He sat there and just looked at me.

"How did Mark Sandberg happen to work for the Williams sisters? Did you ever find out?"

"Sure. She never intended that to happen. He took over to help out some student who got sick. Miss Wayman used to match up students who wanted work with faculty and friends who needed temporary help. She was running kind of a free employment agency out of her office."

"I know. I saw her doing it, but it didn't register at the time. That was how she was able to offer part-time jobs to the boys, to lure them to their deaths. So why was it so easy for Marcia to kill the boys, and so hard to kill me?"

"We don't know for sure it was easy to kill the boys. She talked a lot at first. She seemed proud of what she had done, the way she had manipulated and outwitted everyone. The way she was so much smarter than everyone else. Then she shut up and wouldn't say anything more. But she did have complete control to plan their deaths. With you, she had to improvise. The only time she planned ahead was with the sleeping pills. You've got to admit that if it hadn't been for your grandson, she'd have finished you off that night. Running you off the road, well, she only came up with that idea because she happened to be on the phone with Florence, Mrs. Hokkainen, when you arrived for your visit. Possibly she was reminding Mrs. Hokkainen about how many young men had worked for her and wondering again if one of the dead boys had been among them—apparently she'd done that, although Mrs. Hokkainen hasn't confirmed it yet. We have only Marcia's bragging for that detail. Anyhow, then Marcia hopped in her truck and was waiting by the drive when you pulled out."

"I guess it was the same thing with the dog attack. An improvisation. She was probably in the house the whole time. She probably even set the dog on me."

"That's one I don't know about. You left it out of your notes. Tell me."

I did. He sat there rubbing his chin and looking at me.

"She never seemed the least bit sorry for what her dog did to me. That shocked me."

"It shouldn't have. You had picked her out as your best suspect. How come you didn't tell your son about that attack? Or me?"

"Do you blame me?"

"No. I understand. Heather, you are very lucky to be here." And the silly man took my hand and kissed it.

Another time I asked Dennis how Bill Hodgson had died.

"You had it right. She sent him climbing on that snow dump by the Wendell Street bridge. Actually took him there herself. In the dark. Told him Professor Van Blarcom needed snow samples to check for bacteria count. Early in April, the snow was rotting. The kid was too new up here, and he had no reason not to trust her. Breaking through that snow was like falling into a crevasse in a glacier. She just walked away and left him. Then, when the city dozers started pushing the snow into the river during breakup, his body floated downstream. It was just as you said."

Some things I never understood. Why didn't Philip have Marcia transferred to another office on campus? I asked Joan about that the next time she stopped by. Joan said he was totally unaware of Marcia's feelings for him. That seems hard to believe, but Joan says it is so.

"Would you say that Marcia ruined your marriage?"

"Not really. Our marriage was ill-fated from the beginning. And my life, well, every part of a life is important. The time that's left for me is going to be good. I'm going to rent rooms to freshmen from the villages. I won't need to charge them very much, and I will be able to help them adjust to college. I'll have a houseful of young people at last. Katie George is going to be my advisor. I owe the Oysters a great deal. They helped me keep going at a time when I was totally alone. And they didn't ask any questions."

About Katie. During a similar visit she broke her long silence about leaving her husband so suddenly.

"It wasn't so sudden," she said. "After my first husband died, I went back to college. I had a year and a half to go when I met Bob. He had a good contracting business, and he kept promising me an easier life. He would take care of me, he said. You have an idea of what my life had been, from my book. Hard physical work, all my life."

"And did he? Take care of you?"

"In his way. We had a beautiful home, lots of money. He asked me to give up college. I did. We entertained all the time. His friends. My friends were not welcome. Unless they were white. Eventually, I began to invite my unwhite friends in the afternoon, when he wasn't there. But one day he came home early."

"And?"

"I started to introduce him, but he ignored me and walked to the farthest corner in the room and sat down. It was obvious he was waiting for them to leave, which they did. Immediately. So did I."

"I had no idea."

"No one did. I got my own little house back, and I finished college. I have a good job now with the Native corporation, and as you know, I'm writing a book about my Indian heritage. I'm going to spoil the Oysters' record."

"That won't be difficult."

※　※　※　※　※　※

Well, the Oysters certainly aren't clams any more. Joan Van Blarcom—she's Joan Underwood again—is bubbling over with plans. She says she's going to have all kinds of pets again, starting with that piddling pup she introduced to me in the hospital. "You ought to see him now, Heather. A natural sled team leader." She said she'd named him Scot, because Heather wouldn't do for a male dog—but she laughed when she told me. And she's going to buy an airplane.

"I'm not going to waste a single moment mourning the past," she said, yesterday, over the phone.

Easier said than done, I should think. I suppose there will always be questions: what does Marcia think about Philip Van Blarcom's real connection with the boys she murdered? What does Philip Van Blarcom think about his part in the unhappy events? Is there anything he would do differently, if he could? Does he blame himself for anything? I often find myself pondering these things, but like Joan, I am trying to put the past behind me.

Joan drops in regularly, just like old times. During one of her visits she told me that as we drove from the Pump House to the hospital that night, I had raved like a madwoman the whole time.

"Heather, do these words mean anything to you? 'Damn you, Rowland Adams, let go of my foot or I'll kill you!'"

I was stunned. I sat there thinking about those words.

One time Rowland came home from a long trip and found I'd injured my foot, chopping wood—I wasn't supposed to chop wood when he was away—and it was infected. I was limping around the house, insisting I could care for it myself. When he tried to look at it I ran away from him, and he chased me, all around the house … with me screaming and swearing because I knew that removing the bandage would hurt. But he caught up with me and got me down on the floor … and sat on me. He ripped off the bandage and fixed my foot. I told Joan the story.

"Oh, Heather. You still miss him."

"I do. There's never been anyone like him."

"Heather, I'm going to visit you, often, and I want you to tell me about Rowland. Will you?"

I said yes, I would tell her. When he'd disappeared, flying over the Brooks Range, I had been too stunned to grieve, too busy with little Rowe, with finding a job, and then with working and keeping up the old log house, while I waited day after day, month after month, for him to return. To just walk in the door. The deaths of those boys had brought it all back. I had wept, at last, for my own boy, and all we had lost.

Epilogue

April should be like Aucassin and Nicolette, dappled with impromptu lyrics. "Thus say they, thus sing they, thus tell they the tale."

At the time, there were a number of stories about the murders of the three young men in national as well as local magazines and newspapers and even on television. As a result of the publicity, I received several offers from publishers who wanted my book. Of course it was far from finished, but when a large publishing house in New York said they would rather have my notes, in narrative form, and never mind the mystery novel, the offer was too good to pass up. That is what you have been reading here. I don't know whether that finally makes me a writer or not, but I have been paid, and certainly a book with my name on it has been published.

The Oysters also profited from all the publicity, or notoriety, whatever it was. Joan Van Blarcom, who has quit her job and now boards Native students from the villages, sent off a story to my publisher (my contract called for them to look at some of her stories but she doesn't know that) and one has been accepted, with probably more to come. Gwladys and Gwendolyn Williams are working on the definitive cat care book, which they will call *TLC for Cats*. Abby Buffmire has self-published *More Gardening in the Far North,* and like her first book it is a bestseller, in Fairbanks.

Marian Aldrich is deep into *Garbage: Recycle or Die,* and Florence Hokkainen has thrown respectability out the window; she changed the title of her book from *Frontier Lady* to *Frontier Madam,* and she is writing a no-holds-barred autobiography. It starts like this:

> I was the only child of respectable middle-class parents.
> One night my friend Elmer and I were reading a romantic
> book together, when suddenly he seduced me. Realizing no
> decent man would marry me now, not even Elmer, and that
> my parents would disown me, the next day I embarked
> on a steamship bound for Alaska and a life of shame.

It reminds me of a passage in H. L. Mencken's *In Defense of Women.* I must remember to bring up the subject of plagiarism at the next meeting of the Oysters.

Katie George has signed with a small Alaska firm to publish *Daughter of the Yukon* when it is finished. She has developed a style and voice of her own. She immediately engages the reader, with laughter and pathos, in her life on the great river.

The parents of Mark Sandberg found some comfort in the knowledge that their son had not taken his own life, but not very much, I shouldn't think. For the parents of the other two boys it was perhaps worse, knowing that their deaths were not accidental, that someone had wantonly destroyed their precious young lives.

Marcia Wayman has never shown any remorse. She received a life sentence with no hope of parole. Strangely, no family members ever showed up to support her, no Wayman family was ever found by the press, and no one was ever able to able to trace "Marcia Wayman" before she came to Alaska. What kind of history, I wonder, did she leave behind?

I have heard that she is revising her poems with an eye to publication. After all, she is reported to have said, she started the whole thing.

Did she? Aristotle said a tragedy should have a beginning, a middle, and an end. But "beginning" is a tricky word. You think you've uncovered the beginning, the incident that triggered the whole chain of events, and that incident leads you further back to a preceding incident, another beginning.

So when did it all start? When Marcia came to Alaska, or when she went to work for Philip Van Blarcom? When Joan and Philip were married? Or was it when he so generously shared his seed with a number of childless couples? Sometimes I even feel as if I bear some of the responsibility, but in more rational moments I know I am just one of the victims. I think it started in the silence of a heart. Whose heart?

My parents are still living in their own house, but time is running out. I have hired a housekeeper, and now I get phone calls from the three of them.

One weekend Rowe and Andrew showed up with a truckload of insulation and some stair railing. They insulated my garage and put a second railing on my basement steps. I take that as a good omen. Not that the Pioneer Home isn't a great place.

Even without mysteries and murders life is full and interesting. The mayor is finally showing some interest in recycling, and Dennis Wheeler, who likes to tell everyone that I solved the murders, suddenly made lieutenant.

The Oysters continue their monthly meetings, in months with an *R,* and they have picked up a few new members. Dennis Wheeler's wife Raysheen is one of them. Sometimes I suspect her of joining the Oysters so she can beat Dennis to the draw in case there are any more murdering Oysters. However, she has started an autobiography that she calls *Rookie,* so maybe she really has an itch to write. Time will tell. I dropped out for a while, but *"in sanabile cacoethes scribendi."* I'm back at it, cautious, humbled, and less given to boasting.

Dennis Wheeler asked me the other day if I was happy, now that justice is done.

"Justice?" I said. "There's no such thing as justice. Three beautiful boys died. Three families lost their sons, one their only child. An old woman got a few years in prison, where she is happily writing poetry."

I looked Dennis in the eye. "I suppose if you can believe in God you can believe in justice. I don't happen to believe in either."

I guess that kind of talk scares Dennis. He hasn't been around for a week or so. But he'll be back. He's tasted success, and glory. He'll want to know what my next writing project is.